THE LONDON KNIFE MURDERS

VANCE AND SHEPHERD MYSTERIES
BOOK 8

JOHN BROUGHTON

Copyright © 2025 John Broughton

Layout design and Copyright © 2025 by Next Chapter

Published 2025 by Next Chapter

Cover art by Lordan June Pinote

This book is a work of fiction. Names, characters, places, and incidents are the product of the author's imagination or are used fictitiously. Any resemblance to actual events, locales, or persons, living or dead, is purely coincidental.

All rights reserved. No part of this book may be reproduced or transmitted in any form or by any means, electronic or mechanical, including photocopying, recording, or by any information storage and retrieval system, without the author's permission.

CHAPTER 1
MAXWELL ROAD, FULHAM AND BRIXTON, EARLY 2025

"Hey, mister, can I walk with you?"

DCI Vance stared down into the earnest eyes of a boy no more than fourteen. He leant down towards the boy, furrowing his brow in a stern expression. His face was lined with years of hard work and experience. The boy's face was youthful and innocent, yet there was a hint of street-smartness in his posture and demeanour.

"Why's that, then?" he asked gruffly.

"Because I'm scared to walk alone."

Vance's interest was piqued. "Why's that? How old are you, son?"

"See them flowers against the wall across the road? That's where they killed Billy Taplin. He was at our school."

Vance vaguely remembered a sixteen-year-old schoolboy stabbed while returning home alone from school. The case was still unsolved. "Has someone threatened you, son?"

"No, sir. That's not how it works. They just see an opportunity and kill anyone who comes along alone. Will you walk with me to my bus stop, mister? I have to catch the 222 to Hounslow; we've got a match this evening."

The boy's words gave Vance a sense of unease. He had seen

his fair share of violence and crime during his years as a detective, but the thought of innocent children being targeted struck a painful chord within him.

Without hesitation, he nodded at the boy. "I'll walk with you," he said, adjusting his stride.

They made their way across the street towards the bus stop. The boy walked at a quick pace, clearly eager to get out of the area. As they walked, Vance couldn't help but run a keen eye over the surrounding buildings.

"What's your name?" Vance asked, trying to make conversation.

"Trevor Hill," the boy replied, glancing up at Vance with a shy smile. "But my friends call me Trev."

"Nice to meet you, Trev. I'm DCI Vance."

"DCI?" Trevor asked, curious.

"That's right, Detective Chief Inspector. I investigate crimes like what happened to Billy Taplin."

Trevor's eyes widened in admiration. "Cool! If I can get good grades, I want to be a copper. There's too much crime around here."

Vance chuckled. "Just doing my job."

As they reached the bus stop, Trevor let out a sigh of relief. "Thanks for walking with me," he said gratefully.

"It was my pleasure," Vance replied genuinely.

They waited in silence for a few minutes until the bus arrived. Before getting on, Trevor turned to Vance and said, "You know, sir, I've always wanted to be an inspector like you when I grow up."

Vance smiled at the young boy's enthusiasm. "That's great to hear, Trevor. Just remember to stay safe and always report any suspicious activity to the police." He gave him his call card.

"I will," Trevor promised before boarding the bus.

As Vance watched Trevor disappear onto the bus, he couldn't help but feel hopeful for this young boy's future. He made a mental note to check in on him from time to time and make sure he stayed on the right path.

Vance smiled and said, "Work hard at school, Trev; the police need decent lads like you."

He watched the red double-decker bus pull away and the boy wave to him with very mixed feelings. As he walked back towards the vets along Maxwell Road, he looked around. It wasn't an area that he knew very well, but an old classmate of his had become a veterinary surgeon, and Vance needed his expertise. It seemed a decent residential part of the Fulham district and certainly not a place he would have associated with a fatal stabbing.

His chance encounter with Trevor had destroyed the opportunity for quiet thought that he had hoped for. He was fuming inside. If a young teenager was scared to walk the streets of London, then what was the point of him being a police inspector? He pushed these thoughts to the back of his mind. After all, there was nothing he could do right now to make this area any safer.

Instead, he thought of the events that had brought him here on his day off. It had been his turn to visit his sister-in-law, who had recently lost her husband, Rob, in a car accident. Vance, who alternated visits with his wife, Helena, regretted not having known Rob better before the tragedy. Susie's husband had been a well-respected hospital doctor, and that was the reason. Vance's job allowed him little time for socialising, and the same could have been said of Rob. In fact, Susie was adamant that Rob's death was attributable to a tiredness distraction brought on by overworking.

He checked his watch and saw that he had been away for half an hour, as Howard had asked.

He walked into the blue-painted surgery, where he saw an empty seat. A woman in a grey coat was sitting next to it, holding the leash of a small Yorkshire terrier. The dog bared its teeth and yapped at Vance as he approached.

"He won't hurt you, mister," the woman reassured him. "You can sit down. You're a good boy, aren't you, Tyke?" She patted the little dog on the head.

Vance smiled at her and sat down beside her. "Thanks for the reassurance," he said.

The woman smiled back at him. "No problem," she replied. "Is it your first time here?"

Vance nodded. "Yeah, my sister-in-law recommended this vet for my dog."

"Ah, I see," the woman said with interest. "I've been coming here for years with Tyke." She gestured towards her furry companion, who was now sniffing curiously at Vance's shoe.

"He seems like a nice dog," Vance commented, reaching out to pet Tyke's head.

"He is," the woman confirmed proudly. "He's my little protector."

Vance noticed that she had an accent and asked, "Where are you from originally?"

"I'm from Poland," she replied. "But I've been living in London for over ten years now."

"That's great," Vance said politely.

They chatted amicably until a door opened and a uniformed young woman called out, "Mr Vance, please." He stood to an accompanying snarl from the terrier and walked gingerly past an Alsatian, which remained seated, unperturbed, next to its owner. The inspector had always preferred large dogs and was now about to discover what was wrong with Susie's golden retriever. His sister-in-law had put its listlessness and shedding down to depression and grief at the loss of its beloved 'dad', but Vance was not having that. He noticed the dull-looking fur and lethargy and remembered that Howard had opened this practice. He had always been bright at school, where they had been close friends, but as usual, Vance's line of work had meant they had lost touch.

The vet, in a green coverall, smiled at his old school chum

and said, "Poor Amber has developed hypothyroidism. Have you noticed increased water consumption and lack of sleep, Jacob?"

"It's my sister-in-law's dog, Howard, so I haven't noticed much at all, except that she didn't seem her normal self. I remembered you'd opted to be a vet and thought I'd look you up. Is it serious?"

"Don't worry, nothing that the correct treatment can't contain. But look, Jacob, I'm afraid it's going to be a lifelong condition. Basically, she needs thyroid hormone replacement therapy—it won't be cheap because the active ingredient is levothyroxine sodium."

"I'll take your word for it, pal," Vance grinned.

"I've written a prescription and instructions. But here's a sample to start you off. She'll soon be back to her bouncy self, you'll see." The vet gently ruffled the nape of the dog's neck, and her tail made a listless wag or two.

"C'mon, girl," Jacob said, and the retriever, helped by the vet, jumped down to the floor. The inspector clipped on her leash, and they made their way onto Maxwell Road and over to where he had parked. As he walked back towards his car, he thought about how nice it was to meet someone new and have a pleasant conversation; he had a good feeling of having made a new acquaintance.

He gently urged the dog into the back seat, where she lay placidly as he drove off, thinking frantically. When he found a convenient place, he pulled over and phoned his wife, Helena, who, in their twenty-five years of wedded bliss, had flatly refused to indulge his passion for dogs. She was too house-proud—so it was now or never.

"Hello, darling, oh yes, Susie's alright. It's Amber." He quickly explained the dog's problems and added, "I don't think Susie can cope without Rob, sweetheart, not on her nurse's pay. Yes, I promise I'll do all the caring and, don't worry, goldens are such intelligent dogs, we'll train her not to go into the lounge or on the furniture. You'll see—you'll grow to love her like a child."

He ended the call with a triumphant, "Yes!" then drove to Susie's house. He hoped, correctly, that she wouldn't take much convincing. In fact, Susie was relieved. She loved the dog, but her work made it hard for her to reconcile looking after Amber. The cost of vet's fees and medicine worried her, so she was amenable. "You'd better take her bed and toys, Jake"—she was one of the select few allowed to call him by that name—"oh, and her water and food bowls. There's a bag of biscuits in the cupboard."

As Jacob drove jubilantly away, he looked in the rearview mirror. "You've got a new daddy, Amber!" No reaction. But there was time to build a close relationship with her. Like Susie, he and Helena were both work-committed, so his first task would be to find a willing dog minder. He knew the right person, a neighbour who specialised in rescue dogs. He would be sure to help out for a small consideration. It would also provide Amber with new canine company on Harry's daily walks.

The days turned into weeks, and Vance found himself growing more attached to Amber with each passing day. He made it a priority to take her on long walks in the park, where she would bound through the grass with newfound energy since starting her thyroid treatment. As they strolled together, Vance found solace in the companionship of the loyal golden retriever by his side.

One crisp autumn morning, as Vance and Amber made their way through the park, a sense of unease settled over him. Amber's ears perked up, and she let out a low growl as they approached a secluded area near the woods. Vance felt a chill run down his spine as he noticed a shadowy figure lurking among the trees.

Instinctively, Vance reached for his phone to call for backup, but before he could dial, the figure stepped into the light. It was Trevor, the young boy Vance had met at the bus stop weeks ago.

Trevor looked frightened and out of breath as he stumbled into view. His eyes widened in recognition as he saw Vance and Amber.

"Inspector, sir, thank goodness I found you," Trevor gasped, his voice trembling. "It's my sister. She's in trouble."

Vance's heart sank as he saw the desperation in Trevor's eyes. Without hesitation, he knelt down to meet the boy at eye level, placing a reassuring hand on his shoulder.

"Calm down, Trevor. Tell me what happened," Vance said with a sense of urgency.

Trevor took a deep breath to compose himself before recounting the events that had led him to seek out Vance. He explained how his sister had got involved with a dangerous group in the neighbourhood and had been missing for days. With nowhere else to turn, Trevor knew he had to seek help from the one person who had shown him kindness in this unforgiving city.

Vance's mind raced as he listened to Trevor's story. He knew he couldn't turn a blind eye to this plea. With a determined look in his eyes, Vance stood up and patted Amber's head, silently communicating to the dog that they had a new mission.

"We'll find your sister, Trevor. I promise you that," Vance said, his voice unwavering. Turning to Amber, he commanded, "Let's go, girl."

Without missing a beat, Vance followed Trevor as he led the way through the park and into the heart of Brixton, a locality known for its shady dealings. Amber trotted faithfully by his side, sensing the gravity of the situation.

As they navigated through dimly lit alleyways and abandoned buildings, Trevor's anxiety grew palpable. Vance remained calm and focused, scanning their surroundings for any sign of trouble. The tension increased as they approached an old warehouse on the outskirts of the neighbourhood.

Trevor hesitated at the entrance, fear etched on his face. Vance placed a reassuring hand on his shoulder and gave him a nod of encouragement before stepping into the darkness of the building. Amber followed closely behind, her senses sharp and alert to any potential danger lurking in the shadows.

As they ventured deeper into the abandoned building, Vance's instincts went on high alert. The faint sound of muffled voices echoed from the dark depths, sending a shiver down his spine. Trevor gripped his arm tightly, his eyes wide with fear as they moved cautiously towards the source of the noise.

Peering around a corner, Vance spotted a group of individuals huddled together in a dimly lit room. Among them was a young woman, her face obscured by the shadows, but Vance could sense her distress from the way she held herself.

Without hesitation, Vance stepped forward, his voice firm and commanding as he addressed the group. "I'm Chief Inspector Jacob Vance, and I'm here to ensure the safety of this young woman. Release her immediately, and there won't be any trouble."

The leader of the group, a burly man with a menacing glare, sneered at Vance's authoritative tone. "Well, well, well, look who we have here," he said with a sinister grin. "The great Inspector Vance thinks he can waltz in here and disrupt our little operation, does he?"

Vance stood his ground, his eyes locked on the man as he assessed the situation. Amber stood by his side, her protective instincts surfacing as she let out a low growl. The tension in the dim light grew palpable as the members of the group shifted uneasily, sizing up their unexpected visitors.

The young woman trapped among them cast a desperate glance towards Vance, silently pleading for help. Vance's resolve hardened as he made a split-second decision. With a swift motion, he reached into his coat pocket and pulled out his warrant card, holding it up for all to see.

"I'm giving you one last chance to do the right thing," Vance stated firmly. "Release the young woman and surrender peacefully, or face the consequences, which are serious, believe me."

"Scarper, lads," the burly man cried. "There's too much at stake to risk trouble with the Old Bill."

In seconds, the group disappeared into the depths of the building. A rarity, Amber barked as if to announce a victory. The girl, about sixteen, ran towards her brother, who was profusely thanking Vance. He couldn't study the girl's aspect in the gloom.

"I've said it before, Trev, just doing my duty. Now come on, both of you, let's get out in the fresh air and take stock."

Once outside, Vance said gently, "What's your name, luv?"

He sized up the girl: pretty, slim, no make-up, a natural blonde, no tattoos—just as a girl of sixteen should be, he thought in his old-fashioned way. Even her jeans had no trendy rips.

She glanced for a second at her brother, who nodded.

"Kate Hill. Thanks for saving me from those hoodlums."

"Did they harm you in any way, Kate?"

"No, just threats. It wasn't me they wanted," she said, looking meaningfully at her brother.

Vance weighed up the situation. "If they didn't harm you, there's no need for me to call for backup. But I'll need you to come with me to Scotland Yard. We need a chat, alright?"

The siblings nodded, and Vance walked them and the dog to his car. He dropped Amber off at Harry's place with a quick word of explanation to his benign and ever-helpful neighbour. They shook hands, and Vance drove to his reserved parking space at Scotland Yard. As he got out of the car, he couldn't help but feel there was something unusually sinister about the band of louts in the warehouse.

CHAPTER 2
NEW SCOTLAND YARD, LONDON, EARLY 2025

Vance scrutinised the tense faces of the two youngsters and immediately realised that they knew far more than they had revealed. He did his best to put them at their ease, which was no mean task after walking them through the busy police station.

"So, tell me, Katie, how you came to be a hostage of those toughs?"

"Chief Inspector, I had just slipped to the corner shop to buy some bread, and they surrounded me, telling me that I had to do as they said or they would cut my face." She appeared to be on the brink of tears.

"You're safe now, Kate, I'll make sure of that. You do trust me, don't you?" She bit her lip and nodded; a tear trickled down her face.

"Did you catch any names?"

"The leader—the big one—they all called him Baz, but I didn't get any surnames, I'm afraid."

"What did they want of you?"

"I think they were holding me just as blackmail against our Trev. They said that if he didn't appear before 4 o'clock, t-they would … c-cut my throat." The last three words came out muffled as she began to sob.

"It's all over now, my dear," Vance smiled at her as her brother put a comforting arm around her shoulders. "There's just one thing that I don't understand," Vance said. "How was Trev supposed to know that he had to go to the warehouse?"

For the first time, Trevor spoke. "A young lad gave me a note and sped off on a bicycle—that would've been at about 9 o'clock in the morning. That's how I knew where to take you, Inspector Vance. I've seen you walking your dog in the park several times before but never wanted to disturb you. That is, until today, because I was desperate to speak to you. I hoped you would appear, and it was such a relief when you showed up. I still don't know what they wanted of me."

"Oh, I do," Kate said, her voice trembling. "They were going to force you to join their gang. I heard them talking and laughing about how they would initiate you. They said that to prove you were worthy of being one of them, you would have to stab someone."

"They said that, did they?" Vance's expression suddenly turned grave. "This is more serious than I imagined at first; now I regret not having called my colleagues there and then at the warehouse. My mistake—they would've been under lock and key by now." He sighed, running a hand through his hair. "But unfortunately, they are not in custody and won't face justice for their crimes—not yet, at least," he said with an air of grim determination.

Kate had dried her eyes and was now apparently in control of her emotions. "There's something else you should know, Chief Inspector. I heard them boasting that there was a lot of money to be gained by these stabbings."

If possible, Vance appeared grimmer. "What about your parents? What does your father do, Trev?"

"He's a fitter in a small engineering firm about a mile from our house. I think he works on turbines."

"I want to make it quite clear that neither of you two is in trouble, but I need to speak to your father for your protection.

We can't risk a repeat of what happened today. What time does your dad get home?"

"He usually comes in at 5:30 in the evening," Kate said.

"And what about your mum?"

"She serves behind the counter in a cake shop near home, so she gets home later than Dad."

"We'll drive you home at 5:20 so that I can have a chat with your father."

"Do you have a key, Katie?"

She nodded and smiled weakly. "I can make a pot of tea because Dad likes to have a cuppa and some biscuits when he gets in."

Vance explained to Brian Hill in front of Trevor and Kate that his children should never go out alone for a month or two and the reason. "But they can't live as if under house arrest. I'll have an officer keep an eye on them, and I've told them to ring my number if they are threatened in any way."

"So, they can go to school as usual?"

"Yes, they must. Do you go to the same school?"

"Yes, but I go with my friends; does this mean that I have to take Trev with the girls?"

"You'd better make this sacrifice for a while, Trev and Katie," Vance said, and their father nodded at his son.

Vance, a hardened inspector with sharp grey eyes and a no-nonsense attitude, sat at his desk in Scotland Yard, frustration etched on his face. He had just ordered the files on the Maxwell Road murder brought to him, hoping to find some new leads or clues. However, the investigating officer's note was still attached: there were no witnesses to the crime, and without any new developments, the case had gone cold.

Vance slammed the folder shut and let out a heavy sigh. He knew he needed more information about the streets of *his* city if he was going to solve this case. He reached for the phone, intent on making some calls and gathering intel. But before he could dial a number, there was a knock on his door.

"Come in," he called out, curious as to who would be visiting him at this late hour.

The door swung open to reveal a tall, slender figure, clad in a long coat and a fedora pulled low over their face. They walked into Vance's office, the sound of their footsteps echoing through the quiet room.

"Can I help you?" Vance asked, eyeing the stranger cautiously. He didn't expect visitors at this time, especially not ones who looked like they had just stepped out of a film noir. The stranger remained silent for a moment, their face still obscured by the shadow of the hat. Then, with a voice as smooth as velvet, they spoke.

"I believe you're looking for information on the Maxwell Road murder," the stranger said, their tone confident.

Vance's interest was piqued. "And how do you know that?" he inquired, leaning back in his chair.

The mysterious figure took a few steps closer, finally allowing Vance to see their features. It was a woman, her striking blue eyes meeting his gaze with an intensity that thoroughly intrigued him.

"I have my ways," she replied cryptically. "But I assure you, Chief Inspector Vance, I can offer you the information you seek. However, it won't come without a price."

Vance studied her carefully, weighing his options. He was no stranger to making deals in the name of justice.

"It's an art thief," she said, "Lucas Cadwallender by name. I've been on his trail for months, but he always seems to be one step ahead of me. I need someone with your skills and resources to finally bring him to justice."

He leaned back in his chair, considering her request. Lucas Cadwallender was a name that sent ripples through the underground art world, and if he could help bring him down, it would be a feather in his cap.

"I'll need more information," he stated firmly. "Where was

the last place you spotted him? And what makes you think I can succeed where others have failed?"

The woman's eyes sparkled with determination as she leaned in closer, her voice now a mere whisper. "I know of a gala evening happening tomorrow night at the Grand Rose Art Gallery. Cadwallender has been eyeing a rare diamond necklace on display there, and I believe he'll make his move then. You have the expertise to outsmart him and the connections to ensure he doesn't slip through our fingers."

Vance nodded thoughtfully, already formulating a plan in his mind. The Grand Rose Art Gallery was a prestigious venue, known for its high-security measures and valuable exhibitions. If Lucas Cadwallender was indeed planning a heist there, he knew he had to act fast.

"Alright," he said decisively, standing up from his desk. "I'll meet you at the gallery tomorrow night. We'll catch Cadwallender in the act and finally put an end to his criminal escapades."

The woman smiled, a glimmer of hope in her eyes. "Thank you, Chief Inspector. I knew I could count on you."

As she turned to leave, Vance called out, "Wait. What's your name?"

She paused in the doorway, looking back at him with a mysterious smile. "You can call me Selene."

And with that, Selene disappeared into the night, leaving Vance with a renewed sense of purpose. The hunt for Lucas Cadwallender was on, and this time, Vance was determined to emerge victorious. It was, after all, part of his job, but not as pressing as the murders. If this curious woman, Selene, could supply him with a crucial lead, he'd kill two birds with one stone.

Vance spent the following day meticulously planning the operation at the Grand Rose Art Gallery. He arranged for additional security measures to be put in place, ensuring that there would be no room for error when it came to apprehending Lucas Cadwallender. As night fell and the gala evening commenced, Vance found himself scanning the crowd for any signs of the notorious art thief.

Suddenly, his sharp grey eyes caught a glimpse of a figure skulking in the shadows near the exhibit showcasing the rare diamond necklace. It was Lucas Cadwallender, his eyes gleaming with avarice as he assessed the security measures in place. Vance signalled to his team discreetly, positioning them strategically around the gallery.

As Cadwallender made his move, Vance and his team sprang into action. A thrilling game of cat and mouse ensued throughout the hallowed halls of the Grand Rose Art Gallery. Cadwallender proved to be a formidable opponent, using every trick in his arsenal to evade capture. But Vance was relentless, anticipating the thief's every move and countering with precision and expertise. The chase led them through the maze of corridors and galleries, the tension palpable in the air as each step brought them closer to a climactic showdown.

Finally, in a daring move, Cadwallender made a break for the main entrance, the coveted diamond necklace clutched tightly in his hand. Vance was hot on his heels, determination burning in his eyes as he closed the gap between them. With a burst of speed, he lunged forward, tackling Cadwallender to the ground just as he reached the threshold of freedom.

The necklace clattered to the floor, its precious gems catching the light and scattering a kaleidoscope of colours across the marble tiles. Vance wrestled his captive into handcuffs, his team quickly moving in to secure the infamous art thief once and for all.

As he was escorted away, Vance allowed himself a moment to catch his breath, the rush of adrenaline slowly ebbing away. He glanced around the museum, taking in the chaos of the evening's events. Amidst the commotion, his eyes met Selene's across the room, a silent acknowledgment passing between them. She had kept her end of the deal, providing him with the vital information needed to bring Cadwallender to justice.

As the last echoes of the night faded away and the museum returned to a semblance of order, Vance made his way over to Selene. She stood by one of the gallery windows, gazing out at the city below with a contemplative expression.

"You did well tonight," Vance said, standing beside her. "We managed to apprehend Cadwallender thanks to your help."

Selene turned to him, a small smile playing on her lips. "It was a team effort," she replied. "I merely provided the tip; you and your team executed the plan flawlessly."

Vance studied her for a moment, struck by her unwavering resolve and engaging, intelligent eyes.

"Who exactly are you, Selene?"

"Selene McPherson, Private Investigator. DCI Vance, I'd prefer not to reveal my client's name at this point, but she's a good person and wanted to protect her heirloom at all costs without revealing her identity even to the curator here. I'm merely an intermediary. But listen, I struck a deal with you. The Maxwell Road murder—it was committed by a youth, but there's an organisation behind the knife murders. The ultimate responsibility you'll find in the Inns of Court."

"A barrister!" Vance searched her face, but her lips were tight, and she'd say no more. "Thanks for the tip, Ms McPherson." He knew he would get no more out of her, but in any case, her affirmation bordered on the insane. He would just have to revel in his arrest of the notorious Cadwallender. As he walked away, a momentary spark of reason struck him. What had she said, *it was committed by a youth*. Well, that tied in very much with what Kate Hill had told him. But that an organisation headed by a KC was behind it struck him as absurd and not worth considering.

With clenched jaw, he strode out of his office, almost bumping into a woman officer. He apologised and smiled at the worried constable before heading to Max Wright's workstation.

"Evening, Max, I need the stats about knife assaults for 2022 to the present day as soon as you can."

"Okay, boss, but it's not straightforward."

"Why?"

"Because I'll have to correlate the Met statistics with those of the City of London Police, and then there's the British Transport Police to consider. But I'll see how quickly I can dig them out for you."

"Get on with it, then, there's a good lad. I'll send you a coffee if that helps."

"Undoubtedly, thanks."

Vance worked late, staring aghast at the statistics that DS Wright had provided him. The alarming pace of violence had peaked in May 2023 when three knife murders occurred in just over eight hours. In the first six months of that year, 53 homicides were recorded, and 103 for the whole year. Vance groaned; Trev's schoolmate was reduced to becoming just one statistic among the many.

He realised that it was not just a question of numbers but also who made up those figures. He discovered, after careful research, that 43% of the 2023 victims were white and 36% black, which was a reversal of the previous year's trend. Males made up 81.55% of the victims and 93% of the offenders. This was all very worrying, but what concerned him most were the police statistics: in 2023, of the 103 homicides, five cases were solved, 73 were awaiting trial, and six suspects had died, while 19 cases remained unsolved. He went on to study locations and area poverty levels—those parts of the city facing economic hardship.

Vance yawned and scratched the nape of his neck. He hated dry statistics and had every sympathy with Mark Twain, who famously declared that there were three kinds of lies: lies, damned lies, and statistics. Yet, there was an inescapable truth underlying his research, best represented by the wreath and flowers he had seen for himself on Maxwell Road, dedicated to a sixteen-year-old, innocently walking home from school. This sentiment made him reach for a blank sheet of paper on which he wrote his conclusions about the research.

He wrote:

1. *Despite an overall improvement in the number of homicides being committed in London, the problem of violence continues to affect the city. The high number of stabbings, the overrepresentation of black individuals as victims and offenders, and the concentration of these incidents in certain areas like Croydon, Hounslow, and Lambeth indicate that tackling this issue needs more than just police action. A broader approach is necessary, one that looks at social and economic problems and works to improve community relations, especially among young people.*
2. *Many offenders are young. This highlights the need for programmes aimed at young people, like better education and community support, to prevent them from getting involved in violence. Also, the justice system needs to be more efficient. Many cases are still waiting to be tried, which suggests that the legal process needs to be faster and more effective.*
3. *Reducing violence in London requires a joint effort from the police, social services, schools, and community organisations. Focusing on the specific needs of the most affected areas and investing in young people can help lower these crime rates. This strategy is not just about dealing with the current situation but also about building a safer and more stable future for the city.*

The chief inspector sat back and read through his conclusions again. "Incontrovertible," he muttered, but something niggled at the back of his mind. He reached for his desk phone and called his trusted colleague, DCI Brittany Shepherd.

She breezed into his office and greeted him with a wide smile. Just seeing her so buoyant made him feel a lot better.

"Take a seat, Brittany, fancy a single malt? I need to get your input on an unsettling problem." He rapidly explained his fortuitous encounter with Trevor Hill and, successively, his sister Katie. He pushed a disorderly, scribbled sheet of stabbing statistics for her to consider while he poured out two measures of Lagavulin single malt. He could sense that she was as disturbed as he had been by the figures in front of her. As they savoured the peaty liquor, he passed her the sheet with his conclusions. Shepherd read them with interest, and when she had finished, she raised her head and fixed him with a sapphire-blue stare. "Jacob, you haven't called me here to read these sensible conclusions, so what exactly is troubling you?"

"Is it the whisky that sharpens your wits, Brittany?" he ribbed her. Before she could reply with a suitable put-down, he explained the encounter in the warehouse. "You see, what's worrying me is the feeling that there's some diabolical organisation pulling the strings behind the stabbings. It may well be in an embryonic stage, but what's for sure is that it needs nipping in the bud."

"What Katie Hill told you about the money is certainly disturbing," Shepherd said. "If there's a financial incentive to assault innocent passers-by, we can expect a new spike in the statistics unless we can bring in a new set of preventative measures."

Brittany continued, "I think we need to start with an investigation into the money and the network behind it. We can't only focus on individual stabbings; we need to look at the bigger picture. The increasing trend of violence in London is a serious concern, and if there's a group responsible for this, we need to find them before more lives are ruined."

He nodded in agreement. "You're right, Brittany. We need to dig deeper and find answers. I want you to start looking into the financial transactions related to those knife assaults—if you can find any. We need to discover who is behind this and how they are funding these violent actions."

Shepherd gathered her notes and stood up. "I'll start on that right away, Jacob. We'll get to the bottom of this."

As Brittany left Vance's office, he knew that they were up against something he had never faced before. The statistics were chilling, and the idea of an organised group behind these senseless acts of violence was a terrifying thought. But he knew that Brittany was the right person to lead this investigation, and he trusted her instincts and abilities. He picked up the phone and called the chief constable's office, requesting additional resources and support for their operation. He knew that they needed all the help they could get in order to put a stop to this nightmare before it claimed more innocent lives.

The following days were intense, with Brittany leading a team of detectives as they attempted to trace any financial transactions linked to the knife assaults. Vance monitored their lack of progress closely, while still keeping an eye on the overall trend of violence in London. He was determined to do everything in his power to make a difference, not just for Trevor Hill and his family but for everyone affected by this scourge on their city. Yet, he knew from the obstacles that Shepherd had failed to overcome so far, that anonymity and lack of witnesses was the hallmark of these crimes.

He became increasingly convinced that the only way that they could obtain a breakthrough was through the youngsters themselves, and so, he decided to visit schools in the most affected areas to encourage the teenagers to open up to him. *Yes,* he thought, pouring himself a generous scotch and staring at his large wall map of Inner London, *that has to be the way forward.*

The schools visited by Vance were immediately receptive to his pleas. The headmasters in educational priority areas were sceptical and even cynical about his intentions and questioned the motives behind his actions. But with time, Vance managed to establish trust with some of the students, who opened up to him about the violence in their lives. They shared stories of fear, loss, and despair, painting a bleak picture of their surroundings.

One story that particularly stuck with Vance was that of a boy named Jamal, who spoke of how he had lost his best friend to knife violence. Jamal's friend had been walking home from school when he got into an argument that escalated into a physical altercation. In the end, it was a knife that put an end to his life, leaving Jamal devastated and afraid for his own safety.

As Vance listened to the stories, he became more and more convinced that the solution to the problem lay in improving work with the communities and young people directly affected by the violence. He started to organise regular meetings with local youth clubs, schools, and community centres, encouraging discussions about the root causes of the violence and ways to prevent it.

He also began implementing a mentorship programme, pairing youngsters from troubled backgrounds with positive role models who could offer guidance and support. These mentors would be available to the youths not only in times of crisis but also for regular check-ins and activities to help them build better connections with their communities.

In addition to this, Vance worked closely with social services and local charities to establish programmes that addressed the underlying issues leading to the violence. These programmes focused on education, job training, mental health support, and providing safe spaces for young people to engage in positive activities. Vance knew that these efforts would not bring back the lives that had been tragically cut short, but he was determined to make a difference in the long run, even if it was the short term that desperately worried him. It would not be long before another stabbing occurred in Hounslow—this time of a 14-year-old girl of Asian origins. While Shepherd and her team worked hard in her community, drawing a blank as far as motive was concerned, everyone agreed that Shamila was a popular and pleasant girl, well-liked and without any known enemies.

Even so, Vance was convinced that he was on the brink of a breakthrough with the youngsters that he had spoken to.

CHAPTER 3
HOUNSLOW, LONDON, EARLY 2025

Jadon Wilcox was grateful for the black cotton hood with just eye slits and a small hole to allow for breathing. It gave him some warmth in this cold, abandoned deconsecrated church. His leader had had the brilliant idea of renting it for the day, which was now almost done, from the church authorities. Jadon was a convinced atheist but had to agree that it would be a pity to demolish such a fine Gothic building in favour of anonymous office blocks. Besides, Hounslow needed as much historic charm as it could get.

Another advantage of this venue was that it lent a certain atmosphere to the gathering of ten members and thirty would-be recruits, most of whom were impressionable teenagers. The venue was a grand deconsecrated church, its tall walls adorned with stained glass windows and intricate architecture. The altar was positioned at the front of the room, with the impressive assortment of knives laid out on top. The members and recruits were gathered in pews, their faces full of awe and anticipation.

The imposing figure in the hooded robe stood behind the altar, adorned with candles and an impressive assortment of intimidating knives on display, their blades reflecting the flickering candlelight. The dim lighting and grand architecture of the church cast an eerie glow on the scene, highlighting his position of power and control. The members were dressed in dark, hooded robes, while the teenagers stood and gazed in awe, their eyes wide and curious. A faint whiff of incense lingered in the air, adding a sense of holiness to the atmosphere. Mixed with the smell of old wood and musty books, it created a mystical and foreboding scent.

The quiet whispers and shuffling of feet echoed through the large space, adding to the suspense and anticipation. As the speaker began his 'sermon', the sound of his deep, booming voice filled the church and bounced off its walls, captivating all in attendance.

Like a hunting falcon, eyeing its prey, his hooded head tilted sideways to allow his sweeping gaze to pass over the assembly.

"Brothers," his voice boomed and echoed solemnly despite his hood, thanks to the magnificent acoustics in the empty body of the church, "you have made a smart choice to come here this evening. The Brotherhood offers you the opportunity to earn money beyond your wildest dreams, and all you have to do is plunge one of these beauties"—his arm swept over the assorted knives—"which we'll give you free of charge, into the body of some unsuspecting passer-by. If you manage to kill them, you will be rewarded with £200. A wounding will obtain £50. The more success you have, the greater the reward."

A voice came from the back of the congregation, "You're mad, the whole bleeding lot o' you! I'll have nothing to do wi' you, and I'm off to the police!" The youth turned and ran down what was once the nave. Jadon's hand shot down to the altar and, in a split second, selected a Japanese military throwing knife. In one vigorous action, with deadly precision, the knife flew over heads and planted itself deep into the back of the fleeing youngster.

"There," boomed Jadon, "that's what happens to anyone who betrays us! My prefects, carry the body here to the altar. I want to make sure he's dead, so that I can claim my £200!" He laughed at his own joke—a sinister sound that boomed around the empty interior.

"I'm pleased with the traitor," he continued, "because it shows you all exactly what a risk you run if you break your oath of allegiance. We'll now proceed to the swearing-in ceremony. Come forward one by one, look at the corpse here at my feet and swear by the lives of your loved ones that you will never betray the Brotherhood. Oh yes, we know where you live and who the members of your family are. They can expect the same fate as this wretch, without mercy, if you let us down. Now, come forward in single file and repeat the oath after me."

As the chilling echo of Jadon's words filled the space, the remaining would-be members of the Brotherhood shuffled forward reluctantly, one by one. Each hesitated for a moment, eyeing the lifeless body under the altar and then the cold, unyielding gaze of their leader.

Jadon watched them intently, savouring their fear. He had always been a master at manipulating others to do his bidding. It was poetic justice that he, tormented throughout his youth by his parents, was now able to control these young minds with such ease.

One by one, they repeated the oath with conviction, eyes never leaving Jadon's hooded visage. Each swore to protect the Brotherhood and risked their loved ones' lives in defence of an organisation they barely understood. The chorus of pledges rang through the church, an eerie symphony filled with deceit and danger.

Once the final member had completed his oath, Jadon raised his hand, signalling for the silence that settled over the congregation once again, and with a sly smile beneath his hood, he clapped his hands.

"Now that's settled," he said in a booming voice that reverberated throughout the church, "it's time to put your new allegiance to the test. Brothers and sisters, take your weapons and leave this sanctuary. Tonight, you will show London what you are capable of. And remember, whatever you do... I can't stress this enough... make sure there are no surveillance cameras trained on the place you. Choose your spot well. Go forth and prove your loyalty, and maybe... just maybe, we'll be one step closer to seeing the Brotherhood rise above all others."

As the youths hurried out of the church, gripping their deadly tools with confidence, leaving behind only their leader and his prefects staring at the corpse of the once-traitorous recruit at the foot of the altar, Jadon couldn't help but smirk in satisfaction. He knew that this was a key moment for the organisation and that if all went to plan, he would be richly rewarded by those above him.

"Brothers, over there are stairs leading down to the crypt. Carry the body there, and he'll find his final resting place," he gloated.

The prefects hesitated at the door to the crypt, for there was no longer electricity. However, Jadon had brought a powerful military torch in his carry-all, in case of need. The gloom in the church had suited his purposes earlier, but now, he switched on the powerful beam and lit up the stairs. "Follow me down," he ordered crisply and led the way, stepping carefully sideways down the worn steps so that he could illuminate backwards and forwards until the party reached the sturdy stone pillars that had sustained the church floor for centuries. Even the hardened prefects, who collectively had killed a score of innocent people, trembled at the sight of the stone tombs. Their breath wreathed in front of their faces as Jadon ordered them to carry the body over to a tomb he was illuminating. "Lay the body on the floor and slide back this stone lid." All ten hurried over to do his bidding, heaving with all their might. Inch by inch, with a grating sound, the stone slab moved until they revealed a centuries-old skeleton, the bones yellowed by time and with the macabre skull grinning up at them. One of the prefects put his hand to his mouth and clutched at his stomach.

"Now, ease him in on top of those bones, face down. I want

my knife back," Jadon's callous tone snapped them all back to the moment and into action.

Once the unfortunate boy was lowered into the sarcophagus and Jadon had retrieved his precious weapon, they set about replacing the lid. This they accomplished much quicker than when opening it because, this time, there was no reluctance—everyone was eager to be out of that dusty, dank, forbidding vault.

As the group exited the crypt and ascended the stairs that led back to the main chapel, Jadon gave a nod of approval to his prefects, who began cleaning up the smear of blood that led from the altar along the nave, towards the now-closed heavy wooden doors.

"Tonight, we have taken our first steps towards legitimising the Brotherhood as a force to be reckoned with," Jadon whispered, more to himself than anyone else. His words were met with hushed agreement from those around him. He could see in their eyes that he had instilled a new fervour in them.

They exited the church and spread throughout the dark streets of Hounslow. Like trained wolves, they set off on their assigned routes, each armed with their deadly weapons. The streets were quiet, save for the distant echoes of nightlife in other parts of the city. There was certainly enough knife fodder to be found, and Jadon wondered whether his new recruits had baptised their blades in blood. He was certain that his prefects would do just that and that his superiors would repay him handsomely. The morrow would shed light on their achievements.

In Scotland Yard, the news of the overnight spike in street stabbings left minds in turmoil. The emergency services had barely coped as they rushed across the city, responding to frantic calls for help. From dusk until dawn, London had been gripped by a deadly frenzy of knife crime.

As Chief Inspector Vance entered the bustling headquarters, he could feel the tension in the air. Officers were frantically checking reports and making calls, trying to piece together what had happened and where they needed to be. In her office, Commissioner Phadkar looked worn and haggard as she rubbed her temples with weary fingers.

"DCI Vance," her voice was heavy with exhaustion as she motioned for him to come closer. "This is a disaster. We've never seen anything like this before."

He nodded grimly, taking in the piles of paperwork on her desk. This wasn't just a matter of one or two isolated incidents—it seemed like half of London had been under attack last night.

"We have teams out all over the city trying to find clues and track down any leads," Phadkar continued wearily. "But so far, we've got nothing."

Vance thought for a moment before speaking. "What about CCTV footage? Surely there must be something from all those cameras?"

She shook her head. "Our tech experts are working on it, but so far, they've come up empty-handed." She sighed heavily. "I fear this is going to be an incredibly difficult investigation."

Vance knew she was right. The lack of evidence so far was worrying—whoever was responsible for these attacks had managed to stay hidden from surveillance cameras and leave no trace behind.

"Do you think it could be gang-related?" Vance asked, voicing his concerns aloud.

"It's too soon to tell," the commissioner replied with a frown. "But I have a feeling there may be more at play here than just gangs."

Vance nodded, knowing his superior was right. He could sense it, too, bearing in mind what he had learnt from Kate Hill.

As Chief Inspector Vance delved deeper into the case, he couldn't shake off the feeling that something was being hidden. Despite the chaos that had engulfed London, there was a sense of organisation to it all. Each stabbing seemed planned and precise, as if carried out by someone with a specific agenda.

The lack of obvious signs of struggle at many of the crime scenes added to this theory. It was almost as though each victim had been lured in by someone they trusted, only to fall victim to a gruesome plot. Vance began to suspect that the killer or killers behind these crimes were not simply operating alone, but as part of a larger group or organisation.

As he pored over reports and evidence, his mind turned to the Brotherhood—an infamous yet elusive network rumoured to be responsible for similar acts in the nineties. Could this be their return? Were they looking to assert dominance over London's neuroses once more?

CHAPTER 4
INNER TEMPLE, CITY OF LONDON, FEBRUARY 2025

When Sir Edwin Carson, Conservative Member of Parliament for the safe seat of Chelsea and Fulham, died in early December 2024, the Brotherhood suddenly noticed the absence of its hooded leader, Lucifer Cartwright. Very few of the brothers knew that Carson was Cartwright; a few others suspected, but by February of 2025, everyone knew for sure—not only by his continued absence but also because it was openly declared in the leadership contest between Attila Hateley and Adolf Neville. Their names, like Lucifer Cartwright, were obviously pseudonyms, but members could only suspect their true identities because the hoods and robes did a fine job of concealment.

The candidates agreed on only one argument: the Carson leadership had been reduced only to black masses and a conservative approach to human sacrifices. He had limited the Brotherhood to only one a year. They interpreted events in the light of this conservatism—Neville stated that the Conservatives had lost the last election due to their Infernal Master's dissatisfaction with his methods; whereas Hateley rubbished this theory but agreed that a radical overhaul of the system was needed.

It was a tense night in the Brotherhood's secret meeting chamber as the members awaited the final vote to determine who would be their new leader. Attila Hateley and Adolf Neville stood on opposite sides of the room, their hoods covering their faces, concealing their identities from one another and the rest of the gathered brothers.

As the time for the vote arrived, the members whispered amongst themselves, unsure of which candidate would lead them into the future. Would they continue down the path of conservatism set by Carson/Cartwright, or would they embrace a new era of radical change?

The high priest raised his hand for silence, his voice echoing through the chamber as he announced the beginning of the vote. Each member stepped forward in turn, placing a slip of paper into the sacred urn at the front of the room. The fate of the Brotherhood hung in the balance as the last member cast his vote and returned to his place.

With bated breath, the members watched as the high priest solemnly approached the urn. His gnarled fingers reached inside and withdrew the slips of paper, placing them into two separate piles. The tension in the chamber increased as he counted the papers and then cleared his throat to speak.

"The chosen leader of the Brotherhood," he intoned, "is Attila Hateley."

A murmur rippled through the room as some members nodded in approval while others exchanged wary glances. Attila Hateley stepped forward, smirking beneath his hood, his chest puffed out with pride that his forthright tone had triumphed.

"Brothers, I thank you for your trust in me," he began, his disguised voice deep and commanding. "We stand at a crossroads, my brothers, and it is time for us to embrace change. No longer shall we be shackled by the chains of conservatism. Under my leadership, we will usher in a new era of power and dominance. I shall set the wheels in motion at once."

Adolf Neville stood stoically on the other side of the room—his hands clenched into fists, regretting that he hadn't been as bold and convincing as his adversary. A part of him wanted to challenge the new leader's authority, to dispute the outcome of the vote and claim his right to lead the Brotherhood instead. But as he met Attila Hateley's gaze, there was a glint of something in those dark, hooded eyes that stayed his hand.

Instead, Adolf Neville bowed his head in a show of respect and allegiance. He may have lost the vote, but he was not one to be underestimated. Neville knew that his time would come, and he would bide it patiently, waiting for the moment when he could seize power and lead the Brotherhood down his own path.

As Hateley began outlining his plans for the Brotherhood's future, Neville's mind raced with schemes and strategies. He would play the part of the loyal follower, all the while plotting his ascension to leadership. The shadows of the chamber seemed to whisper their secrets to him, offering him guidance and assurance.

The members of the Brotherhood listened intently to Attila Hateley's words, their eyes gleaming with anticipation for the changes that were about to come. Hateley's promises of a new era filled with power and dominance resonated with them, reigniting the fervour that had once burned bright within the Brotherhood.

But as the meeting drew to a close and the members began to disperse, Adolf Neville lingered in the shadows, his mind already at work on his next move. He knew that patience was his greatest weapon now, and he would use it to his advantage.

Days turned into weeks, and Attila Hateley wasted no time in implementing his vision for the Brotherhood. The rituals became more frequent, just as the sacrifices soaked the streets of London in blood, as Hateley sought to solidify his hold on power.

But whispers began to circulate among the members, murmurs of discontent and suspicion. Some questioned Hateley's motives, wondering if his thirst for dominance was leading them down a dangerous path. Was he actually aiming to become the next Prime Minister? Others looked to Neville, seeing in him a potential saviour who could lead them out of the dangerous police spotlight.

Hadn't Sir Dominic Aitken, Conservative MP for Rayleigh and Wickford, stood up in the House of Commons last week, demanding more funds for policing to combat the upsurge in stabbings? Some of the more astute members on the opposition benches sensed a power bid in his words: "The next Conservative government will ensure that the citizens of London will be able to walk the streets of the city in perfect safety. The deplorable situation of recent days under the present so-called government will take its place among the vast annals of their constant failures."

The Tory members rose as one to give him thunderous applause and bellow, "Hear, hear!" Among them was the member for South Holland and The Deepings, whose clapping was only going through the motions and whose lack of enthusiasm was reflected in his silence.

Scotland Yard greeted Sir Dominic's words with approval and a touch of scepticism. The police had been starved of funding by successive governments. Vance would have ignored the speech completely, except that very morning, he had received an anonymous typed letter which read: *If you want to get to the bottom of this spate of stabbings, seek an interview with Sir Dominic Aitken.* It was signed *A concerned Parliamentarian.*

Vance couldn't shake off the feeling of unease as he read the anonymous letter over and over again. There was a sense of urgency pushing him to investigate further, to uncover the truth lurking beneath the surface. The timing of it all, with Sir Dominic Aitken's bold speech in Parliament, felt too much like a twisted puzzle falling into place.

With a determined glint in his eye, Vance set out to arrange a meeting with Sir Dominic Aitken KC. He knew he had to tread carefully, as the political landscape could be treacherous, especially when dealing with someone of Aitken's stature. But Vance was spurred on by a sense of justice and a commitment to uncovering the secrets that threatened the safety of London's streets.

As he made his way through the corridors of the Inner Temple of the Inns of Court, Vance couldn't help but feel overawed at brushing past barristers—the most prestigious lawyers in the land. Whispers followed him like shadows, and he sensed eyes watching his every move. But Vance was no stranger to the art of subtlety and intrigue. He navigated the labyrinthine corridors with ease, his footsteps silent as he approached Sir Dominic Aitken's chambers.

The door swung open on well-oiled hinges as Vance entered, the room cloaked in shadows despite the midday sun streaming through the windows. Sir Dominic sat behind his desk, a portrait of authority and power, his eyes sharp and calculating as they fixed on Vance.

"What brings an inspector from Scotland Yard to my chambers?" Sir Dominic inquired, his voice smooth and devoid of all emotion.

Vance met his gaze head-on, undaunted by the aura of intimidation that surrounded the barrister and Conservative MP. "I received an anonymous letter regarding the recent spate of stabbings in London," Vance explained. "It mentioned your name, Sir Dominic, and suggested that you might have information that could help me get to the bottom of these crimes." He handed over the note.

Sir Dominic's face remained impassive, but there was a flicker of something in his eyes that Vance interpreted as fear rather than anger or resentment. The latter emotions, instead, were conveyed in his cutting voice: "Detective Chief Inspector, I sincerely hope that you are aware of the gravity of the accusations you are insinuating by coming here today. As a Member of Parliament and barrister, I am dedicated to upholding the law and serving the people of this country. Any implication that I am involved in criminal activities is not only false but insulting."

Vance held Sir Dominic's gaze, his own expression unwavering. "I understand your position, Sir Dominic. But I cannot ignore any lead, no matter how tenuous it may seem. The safety of London's citizens is at stake, and I will pursue every avenue of investigation to ensure justice is served."

Sir Dominic leaned back in his chair, steepling his fingers as he regarded Vance with a calculating gaze. "Very well, Detective Chief Inspector. If you wish to discuss this matter further, I will cooperate within the boundaries of the law. But I must insist on my extraneity from these events."

Vance nodded, acknowledging Sir Dominic's words. "Thank you for your cooperation, sir. I'll be in touch." He rose and walked out with a curt nod, not failing to notice the look of resentment in the barrister's eyes.

Vance turned at the clickety-clack of high heels racing along the corridor behind him. A power-dressed young woman stopped and said, "Chief Inspector Vance, I'm Sir Dominic's personal assistant, Fiona Meadows. How do you do? Sir Dominic asked me to tell you that he would like to continue your conversation if you have the time."

"Certainly," Vance replied, wondering what had brought about this change of mind. He soon found out, as the barrister's first words were, "Have you ever heard of the Brotherhood, Chief Inspector?"

"Indeed, I have, but I thought that it had died out as the right wing of your party diminished."

"I wish it were so," the barrister replied suavely, making sure to keep every trace of deceit well hidden, "but I think you could do worse than to investigate some of my colleagues on the front bench of the House."

"Wait a minute," said Vance, "are you saying that the Brotherhood is behind this wave of violence?"

"I fear as much, Inspector, as I said." He gazed at the police officer with a sincere expression. "I will do anything to help your investigation move forward. Of course, I have no proof—it's just a feeling that something isn't quite right within our party. You know, I've picked up the odd word here and there, and so forth."

"Sir, could you suggest any name for me to begin with?"

"Good Lord, no! It's a dashed delicate situation, as I'm sure you'll understand, old chap."

"You've certainly given me food for thought, Sir Dominic, and I thank you for that."

"Think nothing of it, Chief Inspector. Don't hesitate to contact me if you think it necessary."

"A good day to you, Sir Dominic."

Unfortunately, Vance could not see through closed doors; otherwise, he would've seen the unpleasant smirk on the barrister's face, which would certainly have given him further mental nourishment.

As he left the Inns of Court at a brisk stride, Vance decided that maybe his colleague, Brittany Shepherd, might be better suited to interviewing the hoary Conservative front benchers. As the Force's sweetheart, she had all the attributes for catching elderly gentlemen off their guard. Vance was well aware that his formidable, sometimes intimidating, presence was inclined to raise rather than lower barricades. Undoubtedly, Shepherd was a better call, so he'd return to Scotland Yard and bring her up-to-date with his findings. Something had to be done urgently to put an end to the reign of terror on the London streets.

He knew that Brittany's disarming smile and quick wit could beguile even the most guarded individuals, so she was the perfect choice to delve further into the tangled web of politics and crime that seemed to be intertwining and overwhelming London.

As Vance briefed Brittany on his conversation with Sir Dominic Aitken, she listened intently, her sapphire-blue eyes sparkling with curiosity. She nodded thoughtfully as Vance recounted the barrister's cryptic insinuations about the Brotherhood and the potential involvement of his own party members in the recent violence plaguing the city.

"Seems like we've stumbled upon a real hornet's nest," she mused, tapping a pen against her chin. "I think it's time we start digging deeper into this Brotherhood and see where it leads us."

Vance agreed, as ever, impressed by Brittany's sharp mind and intuitive nature. They hatched a plan to discreetly investigate the connections between the Brotherhood and the spate of stabbings without setting off a chain reaction that would rock Westminster Palace to its very foundations.

CHAPTER 5
NEW SCOTLAND YARD, AND THE ATHENAEUM CLUB, FEBRUARY 2025

Vance and Shepherd began their investigation by meticulously combing through historical records, political affiliations, and connections within the Brotherhood. Brittany's charm opened doors that would have otherwise remained closed to Vance, and her ability to extract information from even the most reticent sources proved invaluable.

They decided to split up their efforts to cover more ground efficiently. Vance would focus on gathering information from the streets and underworld sources, while Brittany would use her charm and charisma to infiltrate high society events where she might uncover more about the elusive Brotherhood.

One night, as Brittany attended a lavish gala hosted by a prominent Member of Parliament, she overheard hushed conversations alluding to a clandestine meeting that would take place at an undisclosed location. "We'll discuss it further at the Athenaeum." Shepherd referred this information to Vance, who went straight to the Commissioner. Under the impelling circumstances, she was only too willing to pull strings to obtain him a membership card.

Meanwhile, Vance's inquiries on the streets led him to a shadowy figure with ties to organised crime who, although his information was of little concrete use, suggested that the Brotherhood were active again, driven by prominent members of the Conservative Party. His patent fear of revealing names impressed on Vance how dangerous and unforgiving the clandestine movement actually was.

As they plunged deeper into the shadowy world of the Brotherhood, Vance and Brittany uncovered a complex web of deceit, corruption, and power plays that extended far beyond what they had initially imagined. The more they unearthed, the more dangerous their investigation became.

One evening, as they pored over stacks of documents in the brightly lit office at Scotland Yard, a knock at the door startled them. To Vance's surprise, Sir Dominic Aitken stood in the doorway, his usually composed demeanour replaced by a look of urgency and fear.

"I've been keeping tabs on your investigation," he began, his voice low and urgent. "You're in grave danger. The Brotherhood is more powerful and dangerous than you can possibly imagine. They have eyes and ears everywhere, even within the highest echelons of government. You must tread carefully, or you may find yourselves in a perilous situation. I can't give you a name with certainty because these people move with hints and insinuations, but a close colleague in Parliament mentioned to me that he'd overheard someone refer to *word on the street* that they were going to take out *the upper echelons* of the police investigations. That must mean you and your lady colleague." Sir Dominic cast an appreciative glance at Shepherd, who smiled demurely.

"So, we're too near the bone, are we?" Vance's tone was icy. "Can you not indicate any names, Sir Dominic? We're chasing shadows."

Was he mistaken, or did he catch a fleeting look of triumph? But if Aitken was involved with the Brotherhood, why was he here at all? Unless it was to warn them off.

"Good heavens, Chief Inspector, the only definite name I could provide is that of my colleague who mentioned what he's overheard. But you must understand that if *we* want more information, doing that would seal his lips permanently. At the moment, it's a quagmire of suppositions and allusions. It would be unwise to rock the boat right now."

"Meanwhile, the streets of London are rapidly becoming a no-go area to the inhabitants." Vance couldn't hide his exasperation.

Vance and Brittany exchanged a knowing glance, realising the gravity of the situation they had unwittingly stumbled into. Sir Dominic's revelation shed a feeble light on the shadowy forces at play, and they understood that they were now in a race against time to unravel the truth before it consumed them.

"Thank you for the warning, Sir Dominic," Vance said, his tone grave. "We appreciate your candour and will proceed with caution."

Once the barrister had gone safely out of earshot, Vance turned to his colleague and said, "You can't fault his poise, but then again, he'll have been to the best public schools and universities in the land—you'd expect such refinement. But, Brittany, I wouldn't trust him an inch. There's something about him."

Shepherd, renowned for her intuition, said, "Oh, so you picked up on that too! I'd go as far as to say that he was warning us off in that elegant way of his." She gritted her teeth and said, "His veiled threats only make me more determined to get to the bottom of this Brotherhood, Jacob."

"I'm with you on that!"

Their first lead took them to a discreet gentleman's club on Pall Mall, frequented by high-ranking members of the political elite—a place where secrets were whispered over glasses of fine cognac and alliances forged in a haze of cigar smoke.

Brittany and Vance slipped into the club seamlessly, blending in with the crowd of affluent and influential men. They exchanged nods with familiar faces, all the while keeping their ears open for any mention of the Brotherhood or the recent crimes that had gripped London in fear.

Despite his pressing anxieties, Vance couldn't resist such a glorious opportunity. "Ah, the good old days!" he teased her.

"What?"

"2001, and they wouldn't have allowed *you* in here."

"You haven't relapsed into male chauvinism, I hope."

"Just teasing, old girl!"

"Bog off, Jacob!"

As he made his way through the opulent halls, Vance caught a snippet of conversation between two well-dressed gentlemen standing near the fireplace. "...the Brotherhood's influence is stronger than ever," one of them murmured, a sly grin playing on his lips. "Our plan to destabilise the city is working perfectly."

He had struck gold! Without missing a heartbeat, Vance approached the men, his posture exuding authority. But he realised that although it was the time, it wasn't the place. Discretion was needed. "Sir, I know who you are. Here's my card. I strongly suggest that you call me at your earliest convenience."

The gentleman's eyebrows furrowed in confusion, and his eyes widened in surprise as he looked at Vance with a mixture of suspicion and distrust. He cautiously assessed Vance's appearance, taking note of his confident stance and authoritative demeanour before nodding curtly and accepting the card.

The faint scent of cigar smoke lingered around the gentleman, mixing with the smell of expensive cologne and a hint of fear emanating from him. Vance made a mental note of the exchange, knowing that their investigation had just taken a significant turn.

As he rejoined Brittany, who had been mingling with a group of influential socialites, he relayed his encounter to her in hushed tones. She listened intently, her mind already spinning with the implications of this lead.

"We need to follow up on this discreetly," she whispered. "I'll see if I can gather any more information from these fine gentlemen without raising any suspicions. Meanwhile, you ponder on our next move."

Vance nodded in agreement, impressed by Brittany's quick thinking. Together, they navigated the elegant setting of the club, gathering what particulars they could without drawing unwanted attention.

Before they left the club, Brittany managed to glean a few more titbits about the Brotherhood's activities and possible connections within the political elite. Armed with this knowledge, Vance and Brittany retreated to the brightly lit streets of London, their minds racing with the implications of what they had uncovered. The night air was crisp and cold, a stark contrast to the heated atmosphere of the gentleman's club they had just departed.

"We need to act swiftly," Vance said, his breath forming misty clouds in the chilly air. "The Brotherhood's plans seem to be advancing faster than we anticipated. We can't afford to waste any time."

Brittany nodded in agreement, her eyes glinting with determination. "Thirty fatal stabbings so far this year… and it's only February. That's almost one a day. I'll dig deeper into the political connections we've unearthed. Perhaps there's a way to expose their schemes without tipping our hand too soon."

"Much depends on the reaction of that politician I gave my card to," Vance murmured, more to himself.

As they walked along the famous thoroughfare with its union flags hanging limply in the damp air, their footsteps echoing against the pavement, Vance couldn't shake off the feeling of being watched. He glanced over his shoulder more than once, scanning the shadows for any sign of movement.

"Do you feel it too?" he asked Brittany quietly.

Brittany's eyes narrowed as she surveyed their surroundings, a shiver running down her spine. "Yes, I do. It's as if we've stumbled into a den of vipers, and they're acutely aware of our presence," she whispered back.

Vance nodded, his senses on high alert. The streets between the pools of lamplight seemed to whisper ominous secrets, and a flickering sodium light cast eerie shadows that danced menacingly around them. They quickened their pace, the urgency of their mission weighing heavily.

As they turned a corner onto Horse Guards' Road, a figure emerged from the darkness, blocking their path. A tall man cloaked in shadows, his features obscured by the dim light, stood before them with an air of menace.

"Chief Inspectors Vance and Shepherd, I presume," the man spoke in a voice like velvet over steel. "I have been expecting you."

Vance tensed, his hand instinctively reaching for his concealed weapon. "Who are you?" he demanded, his voice steady despite the adrenaline coursing through his veins.

The man took a step closer, the dim glow from a nearby streetlamp revealing a glimpse of his sharp features and calculating eyes. "Call me Blackwood," he said, with a ghost of a smile playing on his lips. "I represent a certain faction that is… intrigued by your recent inquiries into the Brotherhood."

Brittany moved subtly closer to Vance, her hand brushing against his in a silent gesture of solidarity. She studied Blackwood with a keen gaze, her mind racing to assess the potential threat he posed.

Vance narrowed his eyes, his instincts warning him of the dangerous game they were now playing. "And what does this faction want with us?" he enquired, keeping his tone firm.

Blackwood's smile widened slightly, a glint of amusement flickering in his eyes. "Oh, nothing nefarious, I assure you. We simply wish to offer our assistance in uncovering the truth behind the Brotherhood and their malevolent schemes," Blackwood replied smoothly. "You see, their reach extends far deeper than you realise, and it would be in all our interests to ensure their plans do not come to fruition."

Vance exchanged a wary glance with Brittany, weighing their

options carefully. The proposal of an alliance with this mysterious faction was unexpected, but the chance to gain insight and resources in their battle against the Brotherhood was tempting.

"We appreciate your offer, Mr. Blackwood," Vance began cautiously. "But forgive me for being sceptical. How do we know we can trust you and your associates?"

Blackwood's expression remained enigmatic, a veil of intrigue shrouding his intentions. "Trust is earned, Chief Inspectors," he stated cryptically. "Allow us to prove our sincerity through actions rather than words."

Brittany spoke up, her voice measured yet resolute. "What kind of assistance are we talking about? This is hardly the place to discuss such matters. Why don't you come openly to our offices in New Scotland Yard? And what do you expect in return for helping us?"

Blackwood's smile turned enigmatic as he regarded Brittany with a mix of curiosity and amusement. "Ah, a lady of discerning inquiry. I must say, Chief Inspector Shepherd, you are as sharp-witted as they come." He paused for a moment, as if weighing his words carefully before continuing. "As for the assistance we offer, it ranges from valuable insider information to more… unconventional methods of dealing with our mutual adversaries, which may explain my choice of tonight's venue."

Vance's eyes narrowed at the vague allusion to *unconventional methods*, his instincts sending warning signals that this alliance could come at a high price. "And what is it that you seek in return for your aid?" he pressed, his tone unwavering.

Blackwood chuckled softly, a sound that echoed eerily in the quiet street. "Merely cooperation in achieving a shared goal: the dismantling of the Brotherhood and the exposure of their abhorrent deeds. Think of us as allies in a shadow war that few are privy to." He inclined his head slightly, his gaze penetrating as he locked eyes with Vance and Brittany. "Consider this an offer of participation in a clandestine dance where the stakes are high, and the dancers are shrouded in darkness."

Vance exchanged a silent communication with Brittany, a wordless conversation that spoke volumes of their shared determination and wariness. After a moment of contemplation, Vance finally spoke, his voice measured yet resolute. "Very well, Mr. Blackwood. Despite flouting all the rules of conventional police procedure, given the gravity of the increasing statistics, we accept your offer of an alliance for now, but know that our trust is not easily earned. We will need tangible proof of your intentions before fully committing to this partnership."

Blackwood's smile widened ever so slightly, a glint of satisfaction flickering in his eyes. "Understandable, Chief Inspectors Vance and Shepherd. Rest assured; you shall have your proof in due time." With a graceful nod, he took a step back into the shadows, his form blending seamlessly with the darkness that enveloped him. "Until we meet again," he murmured cryptically before disappearing into the night.

Vance and Shepherd watched Blackwood vanish into the shadows, their unease lingering unspoken between them. They exchanged a silent glance, each knowing that their decision to align with this mysterious faction would open doors to both opportunities and dangers, not to mention official reprimand.

As they continued on their journey back to New Scotland Yard, neither spoke a word, their thoughts consumed by the enigmatic encounter with Blackwood and the uncertain path that lay ahead. The streets seemed to echo with the hushed whispers of the chilly night, carrying with them an undercurrent of tension and intrigue.

On arriving at their offices, Vance and Brittany immediately set to work dissecting the information they had gathered about the Brotherhood and their strange alliance. The room was filled with an air of urgency as they pored over documents and plotted their next steps.

"This is the weirdest case we've dealt with, Brit, and there's no denying that the Brotherhood's influence runs deep," Vance remarked grimly, his brow furrowed in deep contemplation as he studied the intricate web of connections before them. "But with the aid of Blackwood's faction, perhaps we finally have a chance to strike back."

Brittany nodded in agreement, her eyes shining with a fierce light. "We must tread carefully, Jacob. This partnership may be our best hope, but we cannot afford to let our guard drop. We have no idea who this Blackwood is; why should we trust him? The Brotherhood plays a dangerous game, and we must match their cunning with our own. He could be their emissary for all we know."

"True, another one trying to mislead us, but we've gained time with him, whoever he is. It's up to him to convince us of his trustworthiness."

As they toiled late into the night, piecing together fragments of the puzzle and formulating a plan of action in the face of looming threats and shadowy adversaries, their old partnership, forged over years of knotty cases, grew stronger—an unspoken bond of trust and loyalty uniting them in their quest for justice.

The darkness outside deepened, the only illumination in the office coming from the pool of light cast by the desk lamp. Vance and Brittany worked in tandem, their minds focused and their resolve unbending. Outside, Big Ben struck midnight, its familiar chime muffled by the window but still an audible reminder.

Suddenly, a soft knock at the door broke the subsequent silence, causing both Vance and Brittany to tense. They exchanged a quick glance before Vance rose from his chair and crossed the room to open the door. Standing in the doorway was a figure cloaked in shadows, his features obscured once again by the dim light.

"Blackwood," Vance acknowledged, his tone guarded as he stepped back to allow their mysterious ally to enter. "To what do we owe this unexpected visit? And how on earth did you get past Security?"

Blackwood stepped into the room with an air of confidence, his eyes glinting with a mixture of intrigue and calculated intent.

"Chief Inspectors Vance and Shepherd, I have more influence than you give me credit for, but setting such mistrust aside, I suppose you have been giving some thought to our previous conversation?" He paused, his gaze sweeping over the scattered papers and maps that littered the desk. "I see you have been diligently at work. Admirable dedication, I must say."

Vance regarded Blackwood with a hint of scepticism, his mind still grappling with the enigmatic nature of their alliance. "We have indeed been considering your proposal," he replied evenly. "But we require more than just cryptic messages and vague promises to fully commit to a partnership. We need tangible proof of your intentions and capabilities."

Blackwood nodded in understanding, his expression unreadable as he took a moment to choose his words carefully. "I anticipated your need for assurance, which is why I come bearing a gift." With a flick of his wrist, he produced a small flash drive from the inner pocket of his coat and placed it on the desk.

"What is this?" Brittany inquired, eyeing the flash drive warily.

"A key to unlocking the truth behind the Brotherhood's operations."

"Who are you, exactly, Mr Blackwood? And how can you have access to such material?"

"All I'm allowed to tell you for the moment, Chief Inspector, is that I am the personal assistant to an eminent politician in the current government. Obviously, Blackwood is not my real name, but for the moment, my employer and I would prefer to remain anonymous. That may well change. For now, please evaluate the contents of the pen drive, and I'll return tomorrow afternoon when you've had the chance to scrutinise the documents contained therein. Goodnight, Chief Inspectors. It's none of my business, I know, but I suggest that you both get some sleep." He left as silently as he'd entered.

Vance swore under his breath and rang Security. "Constable, why did you allow our visitor to enter the premises?"

"Did I do wrong, sir? He produced a document with the Prime Minister's signature. It seemed all above board, sir."

"Did he sign in?"

"Yes, sir, with the name Samuel Blackwood."

"That's fine, Constable McArthur, you did well."

"Thank you, sir," the voice revealed evident relief.

Vance turned to his colleague. "Tell you what, Brit, Blackwood's quite right—we should go home and get some sleep. That can wait till the morning." He nodded towards the flash drive. "I'll lock it in my desk."

Shepherd dropped Vance off at his home and drove on, her mind whirling with the day's events, not to mention her unsatisfied curiosity about the pen drive's contents.

CHAPTER 6

NEW SCOTLAND YARD, FEBRUARY 2025

Vance went into the Yard with much the same curiosity as his colleague regarding the contents of the flash drive. However, he was cautious, not being technologically minded, and he warned Max Wright when he handed the device to him. "I don't trust the source of this drive. Make sure it can't corrupt our system."

DS Wright smiled indulgently at his old friend. "I don't think that anyone in the world has anything as advanced as my babies, boss. Don't worry."

"Well, you know best. Call me when you have the contents available."

Max smirked, imagining that it was only a question of moments before he would call the chief inspector. As a sensible precaution, he put the disk through the most sophisticated scans known to man. It came up clean, so he clicked to open it, which brought his first surprise: the drive was safeguarded by a password. Max peered over the top of his glasses—a sure sign of his perplexity—because this was no ordinary password, but a riddle! What's more, it was in Chinese, and despite his all-round brilliance, Wright had no knowledge of that language. Staring at the characters—千里会千金—did not make them suddenly explicable, so he reached for his phone and made an urgent inquiry. He needed DS Xiong Chao urgently. Within minutes, looking rather flustered, the diminutive figure of the sergeant appeared and asked, "You sent for me urgently, sir?"

"Thank you, Sergeant Xiong. I have a password in the form of a Chinese riddle, and I can't read the lingo. Can you help? Come over here." She peered over his shoulder at the screen and chuckled, "It's a well-known riddle where my parents come from—my mother taught it to me when I was little. Let me explain: those characters translate as 'thousand kilometre meet thousand gold'. In Chinese culture, it is said that 'a good horse can run thousands of kilometres per day,' so 千里," she pointed, almost touching the screen with a well-manicured red fingernail, "thousand kilometres is resolved as…" She wrote a character on his notepad: 马, "It means horse." She continued, smiling, "Meanwhile, because a daughter is very important in the family, in Chinese culture it is possible to resolve 千金, thousand gold, as…" She wrote 女, which means daughter."

Max Wright listened, fascinated. He'd wandered around Chinatown in London many times and his eye had swept over the Chinese script in the shop windows, absorbing it only as part of the atmosphere, similar to the pendant red lanterns. Now, suddenly, thanks to his colleague, he was gaining an insight into their intricacy, which became more evident when she said, "The second stage of solving the riddle is visual," she said confidently. "By combining the radical 马… horse, remember," she pointed at the pad, "with the radical 女…"

"Daughter!" Wright said eagerly.

"Yes, together they produce the character…" She wrote on the pad, 妈, which means 'mother'. Thus, the answer to 'thousand kilometres meet thousand gold' is 妈—'mother'."

"Brilliant, Sergeant! I owe you, but don't go away yet. I'm hoping that if I type in *Mother* in English, I'll gain access. If not, you'll have to type in the Chinese characters."

Luckily for Max, the English did the trick, so she was able to return to her regular duties with a spring in her step.

Wright hurriedly printed the three word documents contained in the flash drive and separated them carefully with a paper clip each before hurrying triumphantly to Vance's office, where he found Brittany Shepherd, who had practically taken up residence there while on the case.

At the sight of Wright in his doorway, Vance broke off his grumbling about the nerve of the MP to whom he'd given his card in the Athenaeum Club, who still hadn't contacted him. Vance knew from the sergeant's exultant expression that he was the bearer of good news.

"What have you got for us, Max?"

"The drive contained three documents that I've printed off—I haven't looked at them myself... but something strange..." He went on to explain the Chinese riddle.

"Yes, that is odd," Shepherd interjected, "perhaps the explanation is in the documents... or... well, never mind for now. Well done for initiative, Max, we won't breathe a word to Sabrina." She giggled and glanced at Vance, who smiled. She was referring to Max's wife, Dr Sabrina Markham, Head of the Met's Scientific Department, and to the oriental beauty of DS Xiong Chao. Wright beat a hasty retreat, his previously jubilant expression replaced by the hurt look of an unquestionably innocent and faithful husband. Although, on reflection, he hadn't failed to notice Chao's desirability.

Vance opened the three documents laid out neatly on his desk, the words printed in crisp black ink leaping out at him. The first document was a detailed map of London with several locations circled in red marker. The second document contained a series of cryptic messages written in code, the meaning obscured by complex symbols and patterns. And the third document was a list of names, some underlined twice.

As Vance studied the documents, his mind raced with possibilities. What was the significance of these locations on the map?

Who were these individuals listed in the document? And most importantly, what message was being conveyed in the coded messages?

Brittany Shepherd leaned in closer, her sharp eyes scanning the documents intently. "This is no ordinary case, Jacob," she remarked quietly. "There's a pattern here, a puzzle waiting to be solved."

Vance nodded thoughtfully, his brow furrowed in concentration. "We need to decipher these messages, follow these leads," he said, "but we must proceed with caution," Vance continued, his voice low and measured. "There is a method to this madness, a reason why these clues were left for us."

Shepherd nodded in agreement, her analytical mind already piecing together the fragments of information before her. "I'll start working on decoding these messages right away," she said, reaching for the document with the cryptic symbols. "There must be a key hidden within these patterns."

He focused on the map, his finger tracing the circled locations across London. Each point held significance, he was sure of it. "We'll need to visit these places, see what connections we can uncover," he mused aloud.

Just then, the phone on his desk rang explosively, breaking the tense silence in the room and, as ever, making Shepherd's heart race as she swore under her breath. Vance picked it up, listening intently to the voice on the other end. As he hung up, a grave expression settled on his face.

"That was young Trevor," he said. "Here, I'll lock the documents in my desk and we'd both better hurry over to Trev's house. I'll explain as you drive."

While Shepherd battled with the London traffic, finally resorting to switching on her siren, Vance related the gist of Trevor's message. "The poor lad is terrified. A classmate of his, a certain Chris Costello, turned up in a state at his house and handed over a murder weapon—a knife—telling him to hide it for a few days because he was in unexplained trouble. It seems that twenty-four hours later, that is, this morning, Chris called Trevor again. Their team leader, a certain Baz, has ordered the lad to kill me!" Vance's voice remained flat and unemotional. *"He told Chris that the order had come from the very top of the organisation."*

"The Brotherhood!" Shepherd said through clenched teeth, pulling up at a red traffic light. "It means that they're scared we're closing in on them. But bloody hell, to kill a DCI! The nerve of it!"

Vance nodded, brooding in silence. At last, he said, "Anyway, towards eleven o'clock, Chris called Trevor—this time hysterical and weeping. Apparently, he'd refused to do the Brotherhood's bidding, so they slaughtered his mother and sister right there in front of him."

Shepherd's knuckles became white on the steering wheel as Vance continued, "Baz then said the same fate awaited his father unless he obeyed the Brotherhood's command. He gave Chris the address of an abandoned factory in West Silvertown... turn left here, Brit... where he's supposed to give Chris the plan to murder me... now, that's Trev's house, you go and fetch him while I call in with details about the double murder at Chris's place."

Vance rang base and had a team go to the teenager's address, following normal protocol. Shepherd emerged with both Trev and his sister. "It's best not to leave Katie alone," she said. "Where to?"

"West Silvertown, East End. We're in time because Chris has to take public transport to meet Baz at what's left of the old Rank Hovis Premier Mill. It seems the Brotherhood must suspect that Baz is being followed and that Chris isn't a reliable Brother. By meeting at such a desolate location, they've reduced the risk of arrest to a minimum."

They drove to the south side of the Royal Victoria Dock and parked. Vance told Kate to stay in the car and showed her how to lock the doors. "Don't open for anyone, Katie. I hope we won't be long. Trev's coming with us to identify Chris." The girl nodded and looked pale and drawn. Shepherd added, "Don't answer the radio, Katie, whatever message comes through. Don't use your initiative in any way, okay? Good girl!"

Again, she nodded and watched the trio walk away towards the derelict Millenium Mills, where she could see that renovation work was going on. The officers and her brother gave it a wide berth and disappeared behind it.

The Rank Hovis grain silo, now a listed building, stood behind and to the side of the Millenium Mills. As Vance headed towards 'D' silo, he spotted a solitary figure whom he recognised from the night he'd rescued Kate. It had to be Baz, the tough leader of the warehouse gang. So far, he hadn't spotted their approach. "You two, hang back!" Vance hissed and set off at a run towards him. Vance's heart pounded against his ribcage as he chased after the suspect, alerted by his pounding footsteps, adrenaline coursing through his veins. "Stop! Police!" Vance yelled in vain, but it only fuelled the desperate look in the criminal's eyes. Without hesitation, Baz sprinted towards a rickety metal ladder on the side of the building.

"Stop! Don't be a fool, that's unsafe! Don't do it!" Vance yelled, knowing the danger of climbing such an unstable structure. But it was too late. The man started climbing with reckless abandon, each rung creaking and groaning under his weight, hauling himself towards what he presumed was an escape route. Vance could see the fear and desperation in his face, wondering what kind of hold the notorious Brotherhood had on him: *Bloody fool! He must be desperate. God knows what the Brotherhood have threatened him with,* Vance thought.

But as Baz reached the last quarter of the ladder, disaster struck. The rusted metal gave way, sending both man and ladder plunging to the ground below. Vance watched in horror, as if in slow motion, as Baz's body hit the concrete with a sickening thud, blood pooling beneath him. "No!" Vance cried, rushing over to check for any signs of life. Vance knew this brutal scene would haunt him for years to come.

He felt for a pulse. "Shep, ring for an ambulance!" The thug was still alive, but after a fall of eighty feet onto concrete, he'd be lucky to survive. Vance knew better than to move him; he had to wait for the paramedics to arrive.

Meanwhile, Chris had appeared, looking pale and distraught, and Shepherd was listening to his statement. At last, she told him to go over to the Chief Inspector to identify the body.

"Yeah, that's Baz. I-is he dead?" he asked Vance.

"You must be Chris. I'm Vance. No, he's clinging on. I'm sorry for your loss, Chris, but don't worry, we're making sure your father won't be hurt. It's a terrible business. I hear that you refused to kill me."

The pallid youth, eyes brimming with tears, nodded wordlessly.

"Well, knowing what we're dealing with, you were very brave, and I'm grateful to you. You paid too high a price, but we'll get them!"

His brief consolation was interrupted by a wailing siren as an ambulance screeched to a halt. Shepherd wisely brought Trevor over to Chris, and the lad embraced his friend, and they engaged in earnest conversation.

The ambulance crew soon had Baz breathing oxygen through a mask, and one shook his head gravely. "Officer, you did well not to move him. I suspect a broken back and cerebral haemorrhage. We must rush him to the nearest hospital—that'll be the Queen Elizabeth, through the Blackwall Tunnel on the other side of the river. They have just the trauma services for a case like this."

"We'll follow you there. I'll need to see his documents," Vance replied crisply.

They returned to a relieved Katie, who pointed at the radio in the car. "It's been amazing. I know what's going on. The police are at your house, Chris. I'm so sorry, Isabel was a friend of mine." Chris could hold back his tears no longer, and Katie, sitting next to him, took him to her breast, comforting him.

In the hospital, Vance took possession of Baz's jacket and found a wallet with a driving licence in the name of Barry Holden, aged 32, with a Woolwich address, which might have explained why Baz had chosen the old factory for a meeting with Chris. He knew the East End very well, especially the rundown areas.

Vance and Shepherd waited in a corridor for news of his condition, and it wasn't long before a white-coated doctor confirmed a broken back and an emergency blood drainage to relieve pressure on the brain. "It's too soon to say, but if all goes well, he'll live, but he's condemned to a wheelchair for the rest of his life."

"Doctor, he's mixed up with a very dangerous criminal organisation, so I'm going to place a man outside the door of his room. I presume he'll be in intensive care in a room to himself."

"That's right, Chief Inspector." They shook hands, and Vance made arrangements. He said to Shepherd, "Get me to this address in Woolwich, then take the kids to Trev's home. Chris can stay with you for a few nights, right? Don't worry, I'll have officers looking out for you."

Vance obtained permission to enter Baz's property, a nondescript terraced house that gave no indication of its owner's criminal activities. After kicking open the door and proceeding down a hall with peeling wallpaper, he began his search. Frustratingly, after sifting through piles of old newspapers and empty beer bottles, his thorough search did not yield any useful material. Suddenly, his hand brushed against something hard and metallic under a pile of dirty laundry. He pulled out a gun, carefully examining it. It was loaded. Illegal possession of a firearm at least gave him a charge to pin on the injured man. Even if he had found no connection with the Brotherhood, he consoled himself, he had Baz's mobile phone, which Max would have no problem getting into.

CHAPTER 7
QUEEN ELIZABETH HOSPITAL, WOOLWICH, AND NEW SCOTLAND YARD, FEBRUARY 2025

VANCE RECEIVED A DISTURBING CALL FROM A SURGEON AT THE Queen Elizabeth Hospital. In an anxious, shaky voice, he said, "Chief Inspector, I have to report a murder. Early this morning, I found your Constable Jones slumped, unconscious in his chair. It immediately struck me as strange, and I rushed over to him—"

"Good God! Young Rob Jones, dead?"

"Heavens, no! Drugged. I've taken a blood sample and sent it immediately to Toxicology."

"Thank the Lord! Rob has two young children, but you said you wanted to report a murder, Doctor?"

"Ah yes, seeing the officer in that state—he'll be all right, by the way—I immediately suspected something sinister and found Mr Holden's monitor completely flat-lining. I had visited him around 2 a.m., and his vital signs were perfectly in order. I remember Constable Jones smiling and nodding to me."

"What time did you find Jones and Holden, Doctor?"

"Around 6:30—I'd conducted an emergency operation that lasted three hours: a road accident case."

"Wouldn't a nurse have checked on Holden in that time gap and seen the monitor?"

"That's the curious thing. The night duty sister told me that she had checked at 4 a.m., and both Constable Jones and Mr Holden were alive."

"So, what makes you think that someone murdered Holden?" Vance became impatient.

"Quite simply because somebody had interfered with Mr Holden's drip. The killer had poured a considerable amount of cyanide into the reservoir. I could tell immediately by the bitter almond smell. My suspicions have already been confirmed by our laboratory."

"The murderer entered after 4 a.m., having drugged Rob Jones, and in any case, before you arrived at 6:30. Doctor, this is important: do you have surveillance cameras on that corridor?"

"Unfortunately, our CCTV covers the grounds—for instance, the drop-off area. One does not expect a murder in the hospital, Chief Inspector."

"I'll need to take your statement and have forensics look at Holden's room. With whom do I have the pleasure?"

"Dr Andrew Miles. I'll expect you and your people later, Chief Inspector Vance."

Some minutes later, Vance spoke with Shepherd. "Our best lead has gone, Brittany—Baz was murdered in the night—cyanide in his drip."

"Wasn't Rob on watch?"

"Yes, but he was drugged."

"He can't have been drugged without seeing someone first. We need to speak to him."

"We're all off to Woolwich to catch up on what happened. Sadly, there's no CCTV on the corridor. I expect that patient privacy came into play on that decision."

By the time Shepherd and Vance arrived and parked, Sabrina Markham's team had been over Holden's room with a fine-tooth comb. "There's just one set of prints on the drip reservoir, Jacob, but I should think they'll be Dr Miles's. He's kindly provided us with his fingerprints. He's confessed to unhooking the reservoir and sniffing the cyanide. I think he'd make a good detective."

"He's a well-respected surgeon, Sabrina. Why would he want to abase himself to do a job like mine?"

During the lively exchange that followed, Shepherd spoke to Rob Jones.

"What happened, Rob? What can you tell me?"

"About 4 o'clock, a pretty red-haired nurse took pity on me and offered to bring me a coffee. It was just what I needed to stay awake, so I accepted. It must have been drugged. When I came round, that tall doctor—I think he's a surgeon—had me take off my jacket and roll up my sleeve to take a blood sample."

"What about the cup?"

"Mmm, it was one of those paper cups, but there was no sign of it when I was back to normal. The nurse must have taken it away after she'd killed the patient."

"That makes sense. She wouldn't want to leave evidence. Dr Miles says your blood showed Propofol. It would be easy to access here because it's used in open-heart surgery. It takes effect immediately. We have to find that red-haired nurse. Do you have a weakness for redheads, Rob?" She grinned.

The constable looked flustered when Shepherd's startling blue eyes stared into his. "Not especially, but she *was* pretty and friendly and most of all, the bearer of much-needed coffee."

"We have to learn from this incident. From now on, night surveillance officers must be provided with flasks of coffee prepared by us."

"Sorry, boss. I've let us down."

"Not your fault, Rob. The Brotherhood is still a step ahead of us. They couldn't risk Baz Holden betraying them."

An interview with the Unit Sister revealed that there was no pretty redhead among her staff of nurses. "So, it was an outsider disguised as a nurse. It's not so difficult to obtain a nurse's uniform in a big hospital, or she may have arrived at Queen Elizabeth already dressed for the part and strolled in without anyone noticing," Shepherd told Vance.

"Another dead end," he grumbled. "We'd better get back to base and work on those documents."

In the car, on the way to New Scotland Yard, Vance said, "The one thing that bothers me about that flash drive is why it had a password that used Chinese characters."

"Yeah, I've been thinking about that, Jacob. Did you notice if any of the red marker circles centred on Chinatown?"

"I suspect you're right, but we'll check when we get back."

In Vance's office, they stared at the red circles. They had no apparent nexus, but they discovered that one centred on Gerrard Street in the middle of London's Chinatown district.

"You don't suppose the Chinese are behind the Brotherhood, surely, Jacob?"

"Not for a moment. Knife attacks are definitely not their style. We have a settled, established community, and while it's true that a small minority exploited university students using an application developed in China to circumvent the foreign exchange limit, our Stoke Newington lads broke the ring, and the criminals are now behind bars."

"I remember that case," said Brittany, "because I'm from Manchester and our boys verified that Qiji Wang, a 29-year-old resident of Manchester, was the group's mastermind. At his residence, authorities discovered a money-counting machine, numerous cell phones, computers, and bank cards under different names during their investigation. They were making a fortune out of money laundering at Canary Wharf. So, if it's not that scheme, why do you think Mr Blackwood drew our attention to Chinatown?"

"This marker circle is at Queensway, Bayswater, and this one is Bourne Street, neither of which screams Chinese at me, Shep."

"What do you think its significance is, Jacob?"

"I have half an idea, but I think I'll have to take a closer look to be sure. I'm going on walkabout; see if you can decipher those codes before I get back."

"I can't understand the need for riddles and codes. Once past the Chinese character riddle, why not just explain in simple English?"

"Because if the Brotherhood somehow came into possession of the flash drive, they'd have to struggle through the swamp just like us. Blackwood or whatever geek is working for his faction knows very well that you can trace the creator of a document to an address. Remember how Max did it to lead us to that maniac Declan Drake last year?"

"The Bibliophile killer…oh, yeah."

"Anyway, I believe I've got a glimpse of what that drive is telling us. For the people involved, we need your codebreaking skills, young lady!"

"Oh, just go for walkies, there's a good boy!"

They laughed, but their tension was evident. They knew about the three murders the night before—four if they included Baz. London had never known anything like the Brotherhood's reign of terror. The victims were heterogeneous, which made the case more complex. As far as Vance could see, they were entirely random—people unfortunate enough to be in the wrong place at the wrong time, like yesterday's twelve-year-old in Kensington Park.

As Vance strolled through Chinatown, he couldn't shake the feeling that there was something significant hidden in the red circles on the flash drive. The bustling streets, filled with the aromas of various cuisines and the chatter of both locals and tourists, seemed to hold a clue just out of reach.

Suddenly, his eye caught a glint of a red exterior near a street corner. Walking closer, he noticed a small, inconspicuous shop tucked between two larger buildings. The sign above the entrance read *Li's Antiques*.

Intrigued, Vance entered the shop, the small bell above the door announcing his arrival. The interior was dimly lit, filled with an assortment of ancient artefacts and trinkets from different cultures. Behind the counter stood an elderly man with a kind smile.

"Welcome, welcome," the man greeted Vance in accented English. "I am Li. How may I assist you today?"

Vance hesitated for a moment before speaking. "I'm seeking a connection between Chinatown, Queensway, and Bourne Street. I'm acting on the advice of an old friend, who enjoys being mysterious. When I saw your shop, I thought, *that's what I need, an intelligent Chinese gentleman to help me*."

Mister Li laughed behind clenched teeth, so his mirth sounded somewhat nasal.

"I guess that you and your friend are well-to-do and that you share a taste for oriental girls, is it not so?"

"Ah, so that's Blackwood's game," Vance said, scrutinising the pleasant countenance of the dealer's face as he pronounced the name, but it clearly meant nothing to the shop owner.

"I don't suppose I could buy a little something in exchange for your generous help, Mr Li?"

The man shot a furtive glance towards the door and leant forward confidentially. "Now I know your tastes, sir, I have something that will help you further your aims at Bourne Street." He reached under the counter and produced a sealed plastic bag that contained white powder.

"£100, sir. No need to test it. Li guarantees it. I only deal with top-quality merchandise. If you want it, tuck it away quickly; we can't be too careful, can we?"

"Oh, I quite agree," Vance said, tucking the cocaine into his pocket and telling himself that this sleazy affair was for the greater good. Parting with five £20 notes, he was now certain that he was on the right track. He left Li's premises playing the part of someone who didn't want to be noticed.

Bourne Street ran next to the Chelsea barracks he remembered and was lined with expensive residential properties and the occasional plush office building. He took the Tube to Sloane Square and walked towards the street. With approval, he noticed how clean and well-swept the pavements appeared, which was why a piece of litter caught his eye. It was a calling card and referred to this very road. *London Exquisite Playmates,* he read.

"A-ha, a stroke of luck!" he murmured, because the card provided him with an address and phone number. The street number was a few doors farther down on his right.

Vance quickened his pace as he made his way down Bourne Street, keeping an eye out for the London Exquisite Playmates establishment. The street was quiet, the sound of his footsteps echoing against the elegant buildings lining the road. As he approached the designated address, he noticed a sleek black door with a discreet golden plaque that read *London Exquisite Playmates* in elegant cursive lettering.

Taking a deep breath to steady his nerves, Vance pushed open the door and entered the high-end escort agency. The interior was lavish, with plush furnishings and dim lighting that exuded an air of sophistication. A stylish receptionist looked up from her desk as Vance entered, her expression politely curious.

"Good afternoon, sir. How may I assist you today?" she enquired with a warm smile.

Vance cleared his throat before responding. "I'm here to inquire about your services. Specifically, I'm interested in an upmarket private property which will guarantee maximum privacy and discretion. Money is no object," he said suavely. "A man in my position cannot risk a casual encounter with others in my profession."

"I see, sir," she smiled sweetly. "Any particular taste we should be catering for?"

"Yes, absolutely. I'm looking for a petite oriental partner, preferably Chinese."

The receptionist's smile faltered slightly at Vance's request, but she quickly recovered and nodded in understanding. "Of course, sir. What name is it?"

"Smith."

"Please follow me, Mr Smith," she said, smiling knowingly at the clearly false name, and led him through a curtained door at the back of the reception area.

"Ah, just one thing—do you ladies accept debit cards?"

"Of course, sir."

Vance found himself in a luxurious lounge area, furnished with velvet couches and soft lighting that cast a flattering glow over everything. A moment later, a young woman entered the room, her steps graceful and her demeanour composed.

"Mr Smith, I presume?" she said in a soft voice, her eyes meeting his with a hint of curiosity. She was indeed Chinese, with delicate features and an air of mystery about her.

"Yes, that's correct," Vance replied, feeling a surge of anticipation mixed with unease at the situation he found himself in.

The woman extended her hand gracefully. "I am Mei Ling. How may I fulfil your desires today?"

Vance hesitated for a moment before speaking. "Mei Ling, I'm not prepared to stay in these premises, as I explained to your receptionist. I'm looking for a discreet, preferably luxurious flat where we will be totally private and away from eyes that could cost me my career."

Not to mention Helena—he thought of his wife—*she'd have my guts for garters if she saw me here with you!*

"One moment, sir. Arrangements have to be made. I'll be right back."

As good as her word, she returned after less than five minutes. Her face was graceful and porcelain smooth, with high cheekbones and a small, upturned nose. Her dark lashes framed her almond-shaped eyes, and her full lips held a soft, pink hue. Her black hair was neatly pulled back into a bun, highlighting her graceful neck. A faint hint of floral perfume lingered on her skin. The scent was light and airy, like freshly cut flowers.

She handed him a visiting card, smiled, and said, "My employers will release me after 8 pm when we can meet at the address on this card." Her white teeth flashed as she said, "I'm looking forward to our evening, Mr Smith—can I use your first name?"

"Of course, Mei Ling, it's Archie to my friends."

"Good, Archie. There's one other thing—you have to leave £50 with the receptionist, for administrative purposes."

"No problem whatsoever," Vance said lightly, ruing that his expedition was beginning to cost him dearly. He wondered whether he was entitled to claim on expenses. Gallantly, he took Mei Ling's delicate hand and placed a light kiss on the back of it, wishing that he was unmarried or less of a puritan. Mei Ling was an absolute delight to behold.

He left her and eyed the well-groomed receptionist with reserve. After the oriental beauty, her undoubted attractiveness seemed suddenly banal and terribly British.

"I know you accept debit cards, but since this is our first meeting, I'd prefer to pay cash."

"Certainly. Is everything to your liking, sir?"

"Oh, indeed. Mei Ling is quite delightful. How much should I estimate her fee?"

"She works by the hour. We impose an upper limit, as we have to consider our clients, like you. I think she limits her price to £80 per hour. Of course, tips are always welcome, but not obligatory."

She flashed him a wanton smile, and Vance forced himself to be charming in his leave-taking.

CHAPTER 8
NEW SCOTLAND YARD, EARLY FEBRUARY 2025

When Vance returned to New Scotland Yard, he found Shepherd looking mightily pleased with herself.

"I cracked the code when I realised that I needed to use French instead of English. Look at this!"

She pushed a sheet of paper across the desk for Vance to study. He grumbled because it seemed like scribbles without any sense. She tapped the paper with a well-manicured finger. "Here, look!" he saw the French *homme de ville* and, underneath, in capital letters, CITY MAN. "But that didn't make any sense to me, so when I approached it from a different angle, I got man de ville = Mandeville. Without a shadow of doubt, it refers to the Member of Parliament for South Holland and the Deepings; in other words, it's referring to Sir Charles Mandeville. Wasn't he the man you asked to phone you?"

"Yes, that's him, but surely there must be more?"

"Using the same procedure, I obtained an address, and it translates as…" she pointed to an address in the Chelsea area.

Vance gasped and pulled out a visiting card from his pocket. It bore the address Mei Ling had given him for their evening meeting. He had decided not to go, but this changed everything.

"By the way, Jacob, Sir Charles Mandeville is one of the double-underlined names on the names list."

"Yes, I know. Our respectable Conservative MP has some explaining to do, but that will happen in due course. For the moment, I want to station a photographer outside this address with orders to snap Mandeville entering. Our man will recognise him; he's famous enough after having served as Chancellor of the Exchequer in the last government."

"Excuse me for five minutes, I'm off to see Max. You could make yourself useful and pour us both a stiff scotch. I reckon we deserve it!"

Brittany faked a glower at him as a matter of principle, but she was secretly pleased that he had appreciated her efforts. She wondered how Vance had spent his morning and decided to ask him when he returned. He had been strangely reticent, and how had he obtained a visiting card with the same address she had deciphered? That was curious!

Meanwhile, Vance asked Max to send him the Chinese officer he had used to break the password. The two chief inspectors had just finished their drink when a timid knock on the door revealed the petite figure of Sergeant Xiong, who Vance gazed at in appreciation after his encounter with Mei Ling. He tried not to reveal his jangling red-blooded male hormones to his colleagues and spoke calmly to the Chinese officer.

"Sergeant, I have an undercover operation for you. Have you done plain-clothes work before?"

"Yes, sir, in Hong Kong before transferring to London."

"Excellent! I'm sending you to this address. It's a top-end escort agency. You will say that you are looking for work but refuse to—*ahem*—have intimate relations with their clientele. If you get an opportunity to peruse their debit card payments, do so. I'm looking for those in the name of Mandeville. If Sir Charles shows up in person, make a note of the time. Try to find out how the operation works, especially with regard to oriental escorts."

"Yes, sir, all clear. When do I begin?"

"As from now."

"Very good, sir."

"Another thing, Sergeant. One of the escorts is called Mei Ling. If you get a chance to befriend her, do so. Find out as much about her as you can. Again, if Mandeville is her client, I'd like to know."

Xiong Chau left the office looking very pleased with herself. This made a pleasant change for her from working on community policing.

The night was dark and cold in Chelsea as Sergeant Xiong Chau made her way to the exclusive escort agency. She had chosen her attire carefully, opting for a sleek black dress that accentuated her petite frame. As she approached the discreet entrance, she took a deep breath and pushed open the heavy door.

Inside, the atmosphere was opulent yet hushed. Xiong scanned the room, noting the well-dressed clientele and elegant décor. A tall, impeccably dressed man approached her with a charming smile.

"Welcome, mademoiselle. How may we assist you this evening?" he inquired smoothly.

Xiong maintained her composure and replied in flawless French, "I am seeking employment here, but I have certain… limitations."

The man's smile widened slightly as he gestured for Xiong to follow him. As they walked through the lavish corridors, Xiong subtly noted the security measures in place and made mental notes of potential exit routes.

Finally, they arrived at a tastefully furnished office where a striking woman sat behind an ornate desk. She appraised Xiong with a calculating expression before speaking in a voice that exuded confidence and authority.

"I am Madame Celeste. You say you seek employment here,

but with limitations. Please elaborate," she said, her tone betraying no hint of curiosity.

Xiong met Madame Celeste's gaze unflinchingly and replied, "I am not willing to engage in any physical activities beyond companionship. My skills lie in conversation, discretion, and providing attentive company to discerning clients."

Madame Celeste arched an eyebrow, considering Xiong's words carefully. After a moment of contemplation, she nodded once and spoke. "We may have a position that suits your... particular talents. We will conduct a trial period to assess your compatibility with our clientele."

As arrangements were being made for Xiong's introduction to her potential role within the agency, she discreetly observed the interactions between the staff and clients. She couldn't help but notice the undercurrent of secrecy that permeated the establishment. There was an unspoken code of conduct that everyone seemed to adhere to, hinting at a hidden world beneath the veneer of sophistication.

During her trial period, Xiong deftly navigated conversations with various clients, using her sharp wit and keen observation to quickly establish rapport. Madame Celeste watched her progress with a mixture of approval and wariness, clearly recognising Xiong's potential while also keeping a close eye on her every move.

One evening, as Xiong was circulating among the guests at a lavish party hosted by the agency, she overheard snippets of whispered conversations that hinted at something more sinister than just high-end companionship. References to *special requests* and *off-menu services* piqued her curiosity, and she made a mental note to understand the inner workings of the operation.

As the night wore on, Xiong's attention was drawn to a familiar voice in the crowd. Turning discreetly, she caught a glimpse of Sir Charles Mandeville deep in conversation with Madame Celeste. Their body language suggested a familiarity that went beyond mere acquaintance, confirming Vance's suspicions about the MP's involvement with the agency.

Determined to gather more evidence, Xiong excused herself from the party under the pretence of freshening up. Making her way to Madame Celeste's office, she deftly searched through the desk drawers until she found a ledger detailing the agency's clientele and their preferences. Flipping through the pages, her heart skipped a beat when she came across Sir Charles Mandeville's name, along with a list of cryptic codes next to it.

Realising that these codes held the key to unravelling the agency's illicit activities, Xiong quickly jotted down as much information as she could before replacing the ledger and slipping out of the office unnoticed.

Armed with this new evidence, Xiong knew she had to act quickly. She discreetly made her way back to her temporary quarters, where she carefully transcribed the coded information from the ledger onto a secure digital file. As she worked, her mind raced with the implications of what she had uncovered.

The next morning, as dawn broke over Chelsea, Xiong contacted Vance and arranged a covert meeting at a nearby café. Over steaming cups of coffee, she laid out the details of her discoveries, watching as Vance's expression shifted from curiosity to grim determination.

He explained how he had spent her first evening at another address with the elusive Mei Ling.

"She wasted her first three years in England working in restaurants and takeaways, doing tough work with little reward," she told me.

As she nervously twisted her fingers, Vance listened intently as she recounted her past. Her accent was heavy, and he could tell English was not her first language. He couldn't imagine the difficult work she did before stumbling into sex work at the suggestion of a friend. She explained how it had transformed her life, allowing her to pay off debts and save up for a new house for her family back home. But she only planned on doing it for another two years, wanting to return to her hometown and leave this life behind. The mention of one of her most generous clients, Mandeville, made Vance's stomach turn. When he revealed his position as a high-ranking police officer, Mie Ling visibly paled and expressed fear for what their investigation could do to her. Vance promised her protection if she was willing to testify against Mandeville and offered her a legitimate job with a monthly salary worth £3,000.

He informed Xiong Chao with a tight smile that the woman was prepared to cooperate, and he said, "Along with her testimony and your findings, it changes everything," Vance murmured, his eyes focused intently on the screen of his laptop where Xiong had transferred the encoded information.

"We need to crack these codes and expose what's really going on in that agency," he continued, his mind already formulating a plan of action.

Together, they spent the next few days poring over the encrypted data, using all their skills and resources to decipher the hidden messages. As the words and numbers fell into place, a chilling picture began to emerge of a clandestine network operating within the seemingly innocent façade of the escort agency. Illegal transactions, connections to influential figures, and a web of deceit woven through every page of the ledger painted a dark and dangerous portrait.

With each new revelation, Vance and Xiong realised the gravity of their findings. This was no ordinary escort agency—they had stumbled upon a hub of criminal activity that reached far beyond the glittering façade of high society. People trafficking, especially of Chinese and Romanian girls, emerged while cocaine dealing swelled their illicit gains.

As they delved deeper into the decoded information, they uncovered a trail of corruption that led straight to the heart of power in London. The names of prominent politicians, business magnates, and even some members of the aristocracy were intricately linked to the illegal operations conducted under the guise of the agency.

The implications of their discovery weighed heavily on Vance and Xiong as they grappled with the enormity of what they had uncovered. But they knew they couldn't turn a blind eye to the truth.

Vance consulted with Shepherd, who was astonished at the revelations. Her first reaction was, "Jacob, this is too big for you and I, we have to take it upstairs to the Commissioner. It's the equivalent of an earthquake demolishing the Houses of Parliament."

"I know, and I agree with you. Let's take Sergeant Xiong with us; I'm sure Commissioner Phadkar will be impressed with her work."

"But Jacob, sensational as this is, it's scarcely relevant to the knife murders plaguing the city."

"That's where you are wrong, Shep. Just imagine the leverage I'll have over Mandeville in the interview room. He'll be placed in a situation where he'll do anything to avoid his ruination. He'll spill the beans on the Brotherhood faster than you can say *Bob's your uncle!*"

"C'mon, Jacob, you know I'd never come out with one of your pre-war expressions!"

"I know, you've got a whole library of Greater Manchester expletives refined on the banks of the Mersey."

"Well, I'm hardly likely to come up with one of those in the presence of her Ladyship, the Commissioner, am I?"

"I should bloody well hope not, Brittany. Let's summon Xiong and make an appointment upstairs."

CHAPTER 9
NEW SCOTLAND YARD, AND THE CHURCH OF ST ALBAN THE MARTYR, LONDON, 15 FEBRUARY 2025

By the time Baz had died, the spate of stabbings, the like of which London had never known, came to an abrupt halt. Vance did not consider this to be a coincidence since his officers had made inquiries in the neighbourhood of the deceased ruffian. A picture emerged of a lowlife specimen who had grown up using his fists to intimidate other youngsters. He had been involved in petty drug-dealing and shoplifting, all of which was not particularly compatible with his bank account that showed savings of £150,000.

Vance's realisation set his teeth on edge—Barry Holden was nothing but a puppet, a pawn in the Brotherhood's twisted game of control. They preyed on vulnerable youth, luring them with easy money and promises of power to sell their souls. The recent string of brutal murders may have stopped, but Vance knew all too well that another tinpot tyrant could quickly fill Holden's shoes.

With a steely resolve, the chief inspector made the decision to take down the entire organisation once and for all. He knew it wouldn't be easy, but it was necessary to prevent any future bloodshed. Calling Sir Charles Mandeville's private secretary, Vance instructed him to have the politician come to New Scotland Yard at once or risk arrest and the rumpus of the consequent sensationalised media. It was time to confront the man at the top and put an end to his corrupt empire, even if it meant shaking the Establishment to its very foundations.

Mandeville huffed and puffed, threatening the career of an impassive Vance. He demanded a lawyer, which led the chief inspector to suggest that it might be better to restrict the knowledge of the politician's wrongdoings to themselves if he wished to save his career and his marriage. Mandeville blanched and sat down slowly. "What is it that you *think* you have on me?"

"Let's see. First of all, I don't think, I'm *certain*. We have witnesses to your cocaine habit and your exploitation of young trafficked females. One of the oriental—ahem—*escorts* is prepared to testify in court to your proclivities, Sir Charles; moreover, I have documentation proving your financing of people trafficking and your involvement in the so-called Brotherhood. Let's make it quite clear that we know this organisation is quite distinct from the legitimate Masonic Brotherhood, to which you also belong. To *this* Brotherhood, as I'm convinced you know from what I overheard at the Athenaeum, can be imputed the recent wave of knife killings, and I am determined to bring it down, whatever the cost." He looked at the politician's bulging eyes and sweat-beaded brow and continued, "Your cooperation will help bring about the downfall of the leadership and, at the same time, preserve all that is dear to you; the alternative does not bear thinking about, my honourable friend," he sneered.

"Surely, you can't expect me to face up to the leadership of the Brotherhood. It's suicide! Anyway, DCI Vance, I do not know for certain who the leader of the Brotherhood is—it's true that I have my suspicions—but you see, we all wear hoods and capacious gowns to maintain anonymity."

Vance sat forward, his eyes glinting with newfound eagerness. "This is what you will do… you will inform me the day before the next meeting of the Brotherhood of the time and venue. You'll provide me with your hood and gown… do you understand? This way, you will limit the risk to your person and career, Sir Charles. Regard me as your best friend," he said, the words bitter as wormwood in his mouth, but they had to be said. "You'll see, I'll save your scabby hide! But listen carefully, for the next few months, you'll steer clear of escorts and cocaine, or I'll slam you straight into a cell, clear?"

"Perfectly, Chief Inspector," the politician nodded, the gesture emphasising his double chin. "Now, regarding that meeting, it's on the 15th—three days from now—in a deconsecrated church," he said, standing up and stabbing a finger at Vance's wall map of London. "Here! The Brotherhood rent it for one evening quite regularly."

"Regarding the hood and gown?"

"I'll bring them to you, Chief Inspector, in a discreet valise. Will this afternoon be convenient?"

"Absolutely. Not a word about this arrangement to anyone, mind."

"Of course not, I'm not a fool!" Mandeville protested.

Vance nodded, his mind already strategising the operation ahead. As Sir Charles Mandeville left the room, Vance picked up the phone and called in his most trusted officers. He outlined the plan meticulously, assigning roles and responsibilities with precision. This was their chance to finally bring down the Brotherhood and end the cycle of violence that had plagued the city.

Later that afternoon, as Vance waited in his office, a discreet knock on the door signalled Mandeville's arrival. The politician handed over the hood and gown in a nondescript suitcase, his eyes revealing a mix of fear and relief. Vance accepted the items with a curt nod, his gaze unwavering.

"You've made the right choice, Sir Charles," Vance said coldly, a hint of steel in his tone. "Now, remember our agreement. Wednesday night will mark the end of the Brotherhood's reign of terror."

Mandeville nodded wordlessly and departed the office, leaving Vance alone with his thoughts. The chief inspector knew that the upcoming operation would be tricky, but it was a risk worth taking to dismantle the criminal organisation responsible for so much devastation. As he unfolded the hood and gown, examining them carefully, a sense of impending action washed over him.

On Wednesday evening, Vance and his team gathered outside the deconsecrated church, a sense of anticipation gripping each of them. The plan was set in motion, each officer knowing their role with precision. Mandeville's cooperation had been crucial in infiltrating the Brotherhood's meeting, and Vance couldn't afford any missteps now.

As the minutes ticked by, the sound of footsteps approaching echoed down the quiet street. Vance tensed, his hand instinctively resting on his firearm, buried deep inside his gown, as a figure draped in a dark hood emerged from the shadows. The whispered greetings of Brotherhood members filled the night; their identities concealed by the commodious attire.

Vance watched from a concealed vantage point, his heart pounding in his chest as he waited to mingle with the other gowned and hooded figures. In a low voice, he tested his concealed transmitter, linked to Brittany Shepherd. "Can you hear me, Shep?"

"Perfectly, Jacob. Take care."

He smiled grimly at his friend's anxiety. She was right—this was not a game, but a deadly encounter. Yet, he knew he could take care of himself, not to mention the aid of a score of Met officers concealed in the church grounds and ready for action. Neither did he trust the wily Charles Mandeville, who had not risen to political pre-eminence without considerable Machiavellian skills—quite rightly, because Mandeville had tipped off the leader of the Brotherhood with an anonymous telephone call.

Amid a deathly hush, a tall figure draped in a dark hood stepped forward, his voice ringing out around the abandoned church. His name was Attila Hateley, the leader of the Brotherhood, and he exuded a sinister charisma that even Vance perceived.

Hateley stood before the altar, facing his followers with an air of authority and confidence. "Brethren," he began, his voice carrying a hint of malice, "tonight is a pivotal moment for our cause. We have faced many challenges, but we have persevered and grown stronger."

Vance watched as Hateley's followers nodded in agreement, their hoods bobbing up and down like ominous puppets. He knew they were responsible for countless crimes throughout the city—extortion, drug trafficking, even murder. And now, it was time to finally put an end to their obnoxious crimes.

"You do not know, as I am breaking this news to you now, but the leader of the Brotherhood, Attila Hateley, was sadly involved in a fatal car accident three weeks ago. With his dying breath, he nominated me, Caligula Loathely, to take his place."

A collective gasp and much murmuring greeted these words until the figure before the altar raised a hand for silence.

"It is my opinion," he said, "that our beloved leader was mistaken in applying a policy of domestic terrorism to achieve the noble ends of the Brotherhood. For this reason, I have imposed an immediate moratorium on those activities. Fear not, Brethren, the Brotherhood is powerful and will emerge to follow a legal pathway to glory, always under the watchful and approving eye of our Eternal Master."

Muted cheering was stifled as Vance spoke into his transmitter and a host of uniformed police burst into the former place of worship. Vance pulled off his hood, pointed to the figure before the altar and cried, "Cuff that individual and take him to my office! Allow the rest to disperse and go their own way." The chief inspector undid and shrugged off the heavy, voluminous robe and cast it to the floor in disgust, which Loathely noticed.

As Vance's orders were carried out and the members of the Brotherhood were encouraged to leave quietly, Caligula Loathely was dragged away in handcuffs. The once-powerful leader of the notorious organisation now looked defeated and humiliated.

Vance watched with satisfaction as the Met officers cleared out the remaining members in a swift and efficient manner. He was delighted that violence had not been necessary, and he knew this would not be the last they would hear from the Brotherhood, but for now, they had dealt a significant blow to their operations.

Turning to Shepherd, he offered her a reassuring smile before addressing his team. "Thank you all for your bravery and dedication tonight. We have taken down a major threat to our city's safety."

The team broke into relieved cheers and applause, knowing their hard work had paid off. Vance couldn't help but feel proud of his fellow officers—they had risked their lives to protect their community. Thank God there had been no firearms deployed!

As they began to disperse, Vance turned to his colleague once again. "I couldn't have done it without your code-breaking skills," he said gratefully.

She smiled back at him. "I'm just glad I could help."

Together, they walked out of the church and into the night air. The moon shone brightly above them, casting a glow on their triumphant faces.

But even as they celebrated their victory, Vance knew that there would always be new challenges. The fight against crime was never-ending, but with brave officers like his team by his side, he was confident that justice would prevail.

In moments, the congregated brethren evacuated the building and vanished into the night while, protesting the violation of his civil rights, the leader was escorted to a waiting car.

Once forcefully placed in a seat in Vance's office, Caligula Loathely, the leader of the brethren, began a series of refined threats, nominating the Commissioner, among others. Shepherd stopped him mid-sentence by taking the hood from the angry head of Sir Dominic Aitken KC.

"I knew it was you, of course. I wonder how many years in prison instigation to murdering twenty-seven innocents will get you? The judge will surely be influenced by your betrayal of the robes and wig you wear so proudly in court."

"You cannot prove anything against me, and you heard with your own ears how I have changed my predecessor's illegal terrorist activities."

"Ah, that arrant staged nonsense in the church! It might have fooled your gullible followers…"

"In any case, Chief Inspector, you have no proof against me for your outlandish charges."

"It shouldn't be difficult to follow up on a road accident and find the hospital where your predecessor *died*."

The arrogant, aristocratic countenance showed no sign of concern. Instead, he said confidently, "You had better not detain me on mere suspicion. Your illustrious career, which I have followed with interest, will be imperilled."

"It may surprise you, Sir Dominic, but you are free to go, at least for the moment. I advise you to conduct the policy you suggested to your followers at your fancy-dress party."

The two men would have locked antlers had they been stags, but had to content themselves with reciprocal glares.

The operation had not been a waste of time, Vance reflected; he would now write a full report and submit it to the Commissioner. The *congregation* at St Alban's had seen their leader arrested and would think twice before resuming Brotherhood activities. Aitken had suffered indignity and learnt that he was not as invulnerable as he had presumed. Finally, and most importantly, the lull in the knife attacks might now prove to be permanent.

CHAPTER 10
CHELSEA, 24 MARCH 2025

ONCE DISMISSED FROM VANCE'S OFFICE, SIR DOMINIC, GRATEFUL TO have been spared the indignity of interrogation in the Interview Room, called a taxi and went home. There, he scrambled into his Jaguar and drove over to St Aidan's in Teddington. It would never do to have the cleaners find the robe discarded by Vance the following morning. He was also curious to discover how Vance had laid his hands on what, for the police officer, was the perfect disguise.

As Sir Dominic arrived at St Aidan's, he felt a sense of foreboding. The church loomed ahead, its ancient stones bearing witness to centuries of secrets and sins. Moving swiftly, he slipped inside the shadowy nave and made his way to the confessional. The church was so quiet you could have heard a mouse sneeze. It was there, in the dimness alleviated by the streetlights filtering through the stained-glass windows, that he found what he sought.

The robe lay crumpled on the wooden bench, a silent sentinel of Vance's deception. The chief inspector had dumped it heedlessly on the floor, so somebody had picked it up and placed it on the pew. But as Sir Dominic reached out to retrieve it, a voice spoke from the darkness behind the grille.

"I see you've come for your prize, Sir Dominic," the voice whispered, sending shivers down his spine. "But be warned, there are darker forces at play here than you can imagine."

Sir Dominic froze, his hand hovering inches away from the robe. Who was this mysterious figure, and what did they know of Vance's machinations? With a sinking feeling in his heart, he realised that he was not the only one with a vested interest in the Brotherhood's secrets. Slowly, he turned to face the voice, his eyes straining to pierce through the darkness of the confessional.

A figure cloaked in shadows sat on the other side of the grille, his features obscured by the feeble light. Sir Dominic felt a wave of unease wash over him as he tried to steady his voice.

"Who are you? What do you know about the Brotherhood and its actions?" he demanded, his hand still poised to snatch the robe and unravel the mysteries it held.

The figure chuckled softly, a sound that echoed through the confessional like a sinister melody. "Ah, Sir Dominic, there are webs within webs in this tangled game," the voice murmured cryptically. "Vance is but a pawn in a much larger scheme, a mere shadow cast by the true puppeteer."

Sir Dominic's heart pounded in his chest as he struggled to make sense of the cryptic words. What could this mysterious figure mean by referring to the chief inspector as a pawn? And who was the true puppeteer pulling the strings behind the scenes? Questions swirled in Sir Dominic's mind, each one leading to a deeper level of intrigue and danger.

But before he could press the shadowy figure for more answers, a sudden noise outside the church shattered the tense silence. It was the sound of heavy footsteps echoing from the stone pavement, drawing closer with each passing second.

The figure's eyes widened in alarm, and he leant forward, his voice now urgent. "You must leave, Sir Dominic. The shadows have ears, and they are not to be trifled with," he warned, his tone bearing genuine concern.

Sir Dominic hesitated, torn between his curiosity to uncover the truth and the looming threat outside. With a final glance at the mysterious figure, he made a split-second decision and snatched the robe from the bench before bolting out of the confessional.

As he hurried through the darkened church, Sir Dominic's heart pounded with a mixture of adrenaline and apprehension. The weight of the robe in his arms felt like a burden, a tangible reminder of the web of deceit he found himself entangled in. Every shadow seemed to conceal a potential threat, every creak of the old building a warning to flee.

Reaching the heavy oak door, Sir Dominic hesitated for a moment, his hand hovering over the aged brass handle. Outside, the footsteps were growing louder, accompanied now by muffled voices that made the hairs on his arm stand on end. With a deep breath to steady himself, he pushed open the door and slipped out into the cool night air.

The moon hung low in the sky, casting an eerie glow over the churchyard as Sir Dominic darted between moss-covered gravestones towards his Jaguar parked at the edge of the property. His mind raced as he fumbled to unlock the car door, his gaze flicking nervously back towards the church entrance. Just as he managed to slide into the driver's seat and start the engine, a beam of light from a flashlight pierced the darkness, illuminating his face.

"Stop right there!" a voice shouted, followed by the sound of boots crunching on gravel as figures emerged from the shadows. Sir Dominic's heart hammered in his chest as he recognised their uniforms – they were Vance's officers, undoubtedly alerted to his presence at St Aidan's, maybe even by Vance, who had remembered the robe he had discarded. Well, he was too late; it was *his* now, although he would deny any knowledge of it if pressed.

Without hesitation, Sir Dominic slammed his foot on the accelerator and peeled away from the churchyard, tyres screeching on the tarmac. The pursuing officers shouted commands behind him, but he paid them no heed as he sped away into the night.

As he drove through the streets of Twickenham, Sir Dominic's mind raced with questions and possibilities. Who was pulling the strings other than Vance? What secrets lay hidden within the robe clutched tightly in his grasp? And most urgently, how would he evade capture by Vance and his officers? They seemed to be a step ahead of him. How had it all gone wrong? Lucky that he had a mole in place inside New Scotland Yard, for who else would have made that anonymous call warning him about police infiltration?

His headlights picked out the bridge over the Thames at Richmond, and once crossed, his mind calmed because he was now not so far from his home in Chelsea. Over the river again at Putney Bridge, and he was soon gliding through the streets of Fulham and into neighbouring Chelsea towards his house in Tite Street. He had paid £20m for it, but his financial adviser had reassured him it was now worth £23.8m.

He parked and thought with pleasure how he would now settle into his favourite reclining armchair to swirl a glass of Bas Armagnac 1964. What a pity his wife, Tiffany, wasn't present to console him. She spent more and more of her time in their country lodge in Hertfordshire, and who could blame her? There, she was within a ten-minute drive of their daughter, Eleanor, now a successful fashion designer and model. His career kept him at work at all hours, but he was still in love with her—absence makes the heart grow fonder, so they say. The smooth liquor revived him and triggered his acute mind, which re-ran the events in St Aidan's. The mysterious figure in the confessional had known his name and seemed to be expecting him. What had he said? Ah yes, *be warned, there are darker forces at play here than you can imagine.* And later, had he not intoned: *there are webs within webs in this tangled game* and also, *Vance is but a pawn in a much larger scheme, a mere shadow cast by the true puppeteer.*

The sharp brain of the barrister registered alarm. When he was a young boy, his uncle, a well-known rake cold-shouldered by high society, had told him, on his demonstrating interest in those matters, "Dom, old son, I beg you to have nothing to do with witchcraft and black magic. There are unseen forces in this world that go far beyond your imagination." He remembered what a deep impression Uncle Gerald's words had made on him and recalled every word. "Oh yes, you can sell your soul, but heed me well, His Satanic Majesty will make you pay sevenfold!"

Those words had nipped a nascent interest in the bud, but when he matured and plunged into his successful career, he acquired a thirst for good living and the high life that the city offered. He had been drawn, as if hypnotised, to his first black mass and had been thrilled as he was gradually pulled into the depraved world of satanism, by assisting the rite of human sacrifice when a virgin's blood was offered to the Dark Lord. That was the precise moment when he knew that he had a diabolical purpose on this Earth, one which would also secure him fame and the fortune he craved. He had entered the Brotherhood easily and had risen to take control of the organisation, only to be thwarted by Vance just when the number of sacrifices had risen to the terrifying heights that he sought. He had been forced to terminate Barry Holden, the loyal but limited and self-seeking minion, thanks to Vance's interference. But what did the voice in the confessional mean by saying that Vance was *a mere shadow cast by the true puppeteer?*

The burning liquor went down the wrong way and made him cough and splutter as the barrister's fervent imagination came to the realisation that the description might be equally appropriate to himself. Had a man or a demon spoken to him from the recesses of the absolution chamber? The church, after all, was deconsecrated, so the darkest souls had nothing to fear there.

The revelation that he, Sir Dominic, could also be considered a mere puppet in the grand scheme of things set his nerves on edge. Was it possible that someone else held the strings controlling his every move, steering him towards a destiny he could not foresee? The Bas Armagnac suddenly tasted bitter on his tongue as the implications of this new perspective settled in his mind.

Sir Dominic's thoughts raced back to the mysterious figure in the confessional, his warning echoing in his ears. Could it be that his entire life had been orchestrated by forces beyond his understanding, leading him down a path fraught with darkness and danger? He had always prided himself on being in control, on pulling the strings and manipulating others to his advantage. But now, faced with the possibility that he was merely a pawn in someone else's game, he felt a chill of fear grip his heart.

As he sat in the dimly lit room, the weight of the robe in his hands felt heavier than ever. It was as if the fabric itself held the key to unlocking all the secrets that had eluded him for so long. With trembling fingers, Sir Dominic traced the intricate patterns embroidered on the robe, symbols that seemed to pulse with a strange energy under his touch.

Suddenly, a sound from outside shattered the silence of the room, causing Sir Dominic to startle. He strained his ears, listening intently for any sign of movement. It was then that he noticed a faint glow emanating from the symbols on the robe, casting an otherworldly light around him.

Intrigued and unnerved in equal measure, Sir Dominic held the robe up to inspect it more closely. As he did, a low hum filled the room, vibrating through his bones. The air seemed to crackle with electricity, and he could swear he heard whispers in a language long forgotten.

With mounting trepidation, Sir Dominic wrapped the robe around himself, feeling its weight settle upon his shoulders like a cloak of shadows that whispered promises of power and forbidden knowledge. The symbols on the fabric seemed to come alive, glowing with an unearthly light that bathed the room in an eerie glow. Sir Dominic's heart raced with a mixture of fear and excitement as he felt a surge of energy coursing through his veins.

In that moment, he knew that he had been chosen for something far greater than he had ever imagined. The robe was not just a garment; it was a conduit to a world beyond his wildest dreams, a world where the rules of men held no sway. With newfound resolve, Sir Dominic embraced the power that pulsed within him, ready to confront whatever lay ahead.

As he stepped out into the night, the darkness seemed to part before him, revealing a path illuminated by an otherworldly light. The sounds of the city faded into the background as he walked with purpose, guided by forces unseen but keenly felt.

In the distance, the bulk of St Aidan's loomed before him, beckoning like a dark hand against the night sky. Sir Dominic felt a pull towards the church, a magnetic force that he could not resist. As he approached the ancient building, a sense of foreboding came over him, but he pushed aside his fear and stepped through the heavy wooden doors.

The interior of St Aidan's was bathed in the ethereal wash of pale moonlight filtering through stained-glass windows to cast colourful patterns on the stone floor. Shadows danced along the walls as Sir Dominic made his way down the aisle, the echoes of his footsteps reverberating through the empty church.

At the altar, a figure cloaked in darkness stood waiting. His presence exuded a power that sent shivers down Sir Dominic's spine, but he squared his shoulders and met his gaze with determination.

"So, you have come," the figure intoned, his voice resonating with an otherworldly quality. "The time has come to fulfil your destiny, Sir Dominic."

"W-who are you?" His question went ignored.

Sir Dominic felt a surge of conflicting emotions wash over him—fear, curiosity, and a strange sense of exhilaration. He knew that whatever lay ahead would irrevocably change the course of his life, but he also felt a deep-seated need to unravel the mysteries that had long eluded him. As he stood before the cloaked figure, he mustered all the courage he could and spoke in a voice that surprised even himself.

"What is my destiny?" Sir Dominic's words echoed through the empty church, mingling with the whispers of ages past. The figure before him seemed to consider his question for a moment, their shadowed features inscrutable in the dim light.

"Your destiny," the figure finally spoke, "is intertwined with forces far beyond your current understanding. You have been chosen to wield a power that few mortals can comprehend—a power that can shape worlds and destinies." Sir Dominic felt an icy chill grip him at these words, but an undeniable spark of excitement flickered within his breast.

The voice continued, now with a stern tone, "But you must return to making blood sacrifices to your Master; organise your affairs with care, and the rewards will be great."

"I shall do as you will and move with caution," he replied with certainty. His dream of becoming Prime Minister and a Peer of the Realm had never seemed closer than tonight.

Sir Dominic's mind raced with the possibilities that lay before him, a mixture of ambition and apprehension swirling within him. The figure's words had ignited a fire within his soul—a burning desire to unlock the true extent of the power that had been promised to him. As he made his way out of the church, the weight of his newfound destiny settled upon his shoulders like a heavy cloak.

The city streets were deserted as he walked through the night, the echo of his footsteps following him like a haunting melody. Sir Dominic knew that from this moment on, his path was irrevocably changed. The pact he had made with dark forces loomed over him like a shadow, whispering promises of grandeur and dominion.

Against the backdrop of the dark sky, Sir Dominic's mansion was a beacon of light and wealth. The golden lights shining from every window cast dancing shadows on the lawn. As he entered, he passed through opulent halls adorned with fine art and expensive furnishings. Sir Dominic wasted no time in setting his twisted plans into motion. He grabbed a sheet of paper and scrawled down the names of his most loyal followers, preparing how best to relay the sinister instructions he had received in the church. But then, his gaze fell upon the robe neatly folded on a chair. Something inside him compelled him to abandon his armagnac and inspect it closely. As he lifted it, a wave of dark energy washed over him, telling him that its symbols had already served their purpose for the night. With a determined sneer, Sir Dominic checked the inside pocket—empty. But then, a tailor's label caught his eye: Hargreaves & Jenks, bespoke tailors on Savile Row. It was clear that Vance had obtained this costly garment from one of the Brethren. And so, with a wicked grin, Sir Dominic made it his first task to find out who. Tomorrow morning, he would visit Messrs Hargreaves & Jenks with the robe carefully packed into a travel case. What better offering to his Master than the blood of a traitor? If he could identify and execute this betrayer, Sir Dominic knew he would gain even more favour in the eyes of his dark deity. A malevolent chuckle escaped his lips as he poured himself another stiff drink. The alcohol took its toll, and soon after an exhausting day, Sir Dominic's head lolled against the wing of his chair as he fell into a deep and dreamless sleep, content in knowing that his darkest desires were coming to fruition.

As the morning sunlight struck his yellow curtains, sending a warm glow into the room, he drifted in and out of sleep, dreaming of all the power that he would exercise one day soon.

CHAPTER 11
CHELSEA AND CITY OF WESTMINSTER, 25–31 MARCH, 2025

Sir Dominic Aitken strode confidently through the City of Westminster and turned into Savile Row, where his gaze was caught by a blue plaque that he had not noticed before, affixed to the wall of number 3. He read it: *The Beatles played their last live performance on the roof of this building, 30th January 1969.* He murmured to himself, "Good Lord! That was ten years before I was born. Strange, I've never seen it."

He smiled, reflecting that among older popular music, that of the Beatles aged very well, although he preferred Dvořák with a cognac when he relaxed in the evening. He continued his expedition, conscious of the weighty valise containing the discarded ceremonial robe, which he swapped to his left hand. There was an embarrassment of choice of tailors as his eyes took in the various company names, one more prestigious than the next. At last, halfway down the Row, he came to an elegant façade with a white-framed bow window, contrasting pleasantly with the dark brickwork. Gold letters in relief followed the curve of the window and dominated it from above: Hargreaves and Jenks, he read, pleased to have arrived. Again, he changed hands with the small but heavy suitcase. The property, like the others, was fronted by a spiked black iron railing. He passed through the opening to the elegant doorway with its semi-circular white transom, ridged to look like a lady's fan from bygone times. The black-painted door with its white vertical lites made up of three narrow window panes was architecturally pleasing to the eye. He would have expected no less for such an esteemed business.

As he slipped through the door, he decided to treat himself to a new grey three-piece suit, about which he informed the courteous assistant, who immediately sought a stack pad of fabric samples for him to peruse.

Having chosen the cloth, Aitken allowed himself to be measured, a procedure which bored him but which would reward him with a natty suit for social occasions. It gave him time to work out his approach regarding the robe.

When the tailor had finished, inside leg and all, he said, "I have an item with me, which you might be able to help me decipher."

The tailor, an elderly bespectacled man, peered myopically at the barrister, curiosity writ large on his face.

"You intrigue me, sir. How can I help?"

Aitken snatched up the valise and placed it on a counter, unzipping it to reveal the ceremonial robe. He gathered it in both hands and allowed it to unfold under its own weight. "There, I saw your label stitched inside, and it is of great importance to know the name of the customer who ordered its creation."

"I remember him well. We rarely have an order so—how can I put it?" He coughed discreetly, *"exotic and challenging.* A portly gentleman who, meanwhile, has risen to eminence. I believe he was the previous Chancellor of the Exchequer."

"Sir Charles Mandeville," Aitken growled through clenched teeth.

"Oh yes, you have Jacob Jenks's word—I never forget my customers' faces."

"Well, Mr Jenks, you've been very helpful, much appreciated! Please call me on this number"—he handed over a visiting card —"when you're ready for the fitting."

He began to bundle the robe into the valise, but the tailor clicked his tongue and fussily took over, folding the garment with expert hands until it lay snugly inside the small suitcase.

"I remember, we had to obtain outside help for the embroidery of the symbols," the tailor spoke with a weak, quavering voice, which suggested he didn't enjoy the best of health. "What is it? Some kind of secret society?"

"A Brotherhood of socially minded individuals with the aim of improving life in general. It's better that its membership remains secret. It's essential that I restore the robe to its rightful owner. I fear that it may have been misappropriated, and in that sense, I'm merely a middleman," he lied and cheerfully left the premises with vengeance on his mind. He would find a way to make Charles Mandeville pay for his treachery.

After more than twenty years in chambers, Sir Dominic Aitken had acquired extensive contacts on either side of *the legal fence*. Among the bad boys who owed him a favour for obtaining acquittal when he seemed doomed to a long prison sentence was Martyn 'Marty' Rowell, who had also been an Etonian. His close call with justice had not altered Rowell's criminal activities—they had just needed resetting according to Aitken's cunning suggestions. Rowell was now at the head of a brilliantly organised drug gang and accumulating an enormous fortune. Aitken's system involved handing out drugs by giving out business cards where a line number acted as a single point of contact, whereby marketing messages were sent to drug users, advertising the commodity for sale, the pricing structure, and the dealer's availability. The users would then, in turn, text or phone back with their orders and arrange some means of meeting the dealer to conduct the transaction. Strangely, in recent times, Rowell had become quieter, and the flood of illicit gains into the barrister's account had reduced to a trickle. He needed to get to the bottom of that!

As a serving barrister, this was everything he had sworn to combat, but by now, Sir Dominic Aitken was the faithful servant of the Dark Lord and counted several successful crime barons among his secret friends. In other words, Sir Dominic led a double life. He now needed to call in a favour. He was too wily to use his personal mobile or the office phone, so he unlocked his safe and took out a tray of mobiles, each carefully labelled with a codename. Marty's name in code was *Olden Spur*—a play on his surname, the rowel being the spiked revolving disc at the end of a spur.

Aitken selected it and pressed the only number in the contacts. A suave and most un-criminal voice greeted him amicably, "Dom, old chap, what can I do for you?"

The barrister explained that he needed a desperado, a neighbourhood bully eager to earn a considerable recompense in return for unswerving loyalty and discretion. Among the prerequisites was that he must have already committed murder or manslaughter and got away with it.

"I say, those types don't grow on trees, old chap, but leave it with me. I might just have the fellow—er—*felon* you seek. I'll get back to you within the hour."

Damn! It slipped my mind to ask him for an explanation for the decreased flow of funds. Ah well, next time.

He slipped the mobile into his jacket pocket and proceeded to read through a pad of neatly typed case notes. Part of Aitken still adored his chambers' commitment to fighting injustice, defending human rights, and upholding the rule of law—whenever these high ideals didn't interfere with his secret agenda of ambition and diabolical servitude.

Within the hour, Marty Rowell contacted Sir Dominic Aitken, informing him that he had found the perfect candidate for the barrister's mysterious request. The man's name was Victor Holywell, a notorious figure in the criminal underworld known for his ruthlessness and ability to evade capture. Aitken arranged to meet with Holywell in a discreet location that very evening.

As Sir Dominic waited in a dimly lit alley, cloaked in shadows, a figure approached him with a menacing aura. Victor

Holywell was a towering man with sharp features and eyes that seemed to pierce through the darkness.

"You must be Sir Dominic," Holywell rumbled, his voice low and dangerous.

Aitken nodded, impressed by the man's imposing presence. "I have a proposition for you, Mr Holywell," he began. "Allow me to outline the details of the job I require and the substantial payment that will accompany it."

Holywell listened intently, his expression unreadable. After a moment of silence, Aitken continued. "It must be a totally clean job, untraceable to either of us. I want you to stab to death a politician by the name of Sir Charles Mandeville. You'll have heard of him. It's up to you to find him, choose a discreet place and do the deed, in return for which you'll receive £25,000—£5,000 now, in used notes, and the rest on completion, which must be within the month of March."

Sir Dominic's mouth twitched upwards at one corner as the ruffian snatched the padded envelope and tucked it in his coat. "I'll check this at home," he growled. The barrister took out two small, functional mobile phones. "Here, there's only one number. Only use this to contact me on this one reserved for your calls and messages. Don't let me down, Victor, or even dream of betraying me: I'm even more dangerous than you!"

"Don't worry about that, your target's as good as dead."

Sir Dominic watched as Victor Holywell disappeared into the night, his formidable figure blending seamlessly with the darkness. A cold shiver coursed down Aitken's spine, a mixture of excitement and dread at what he had set in motion. As he made his way back to his chambers, his mind raced with the possibilities of what was to come. He would now pray to his satanic overlord and offer up Sir Charles Mandeville as a sacrifice.

Weeks passed, and the deadline for the politician's demise drew closer. Aitken received sporadic updates from Holywell through their secure line, each message cryptic and vague, leaving Aitken on edge with anticipation. Finally, on a chilly

March evening, Aitken's phone buzzed with a single word: "Done."

A rush of exhilaration flooded through Sir Dominic as he realised his plan had come to fruition. The following morning's newspapers confirmed the headlines he had been eagerly awaiting: Prominent Politician Brutally Slain in Mysterious Murder. A smirk played on Aitken's lips as he read how the bloodied corpse had been found in a public toilet with his throat cut and his trousers down around his ankles. "I didn't know you cultivated that particular vice, old boy!" Sir Dominic smirked, taking Holywell's private mobile from his collection and sending a text organising the location to make the outstanding payment.

They met in the same dark alley, where few ventured at night. It was so creepy that Aitken was relieved to see the formidable figure of Holywell appear right on time. No form of lowlife would dare mug him for his wallet or his special package, which burnt his hand as if red-hot, while the killer was around.

"How did you find out he had a taste for rent boys?"

"Word soon gets around in certain places I frequent. I put out a few feelers and made the discovery. From there, it was easy to set up an amorous encounter. Not that I'm that way inclined, boss."

"Me neither, but it turned out to be a clever move. I'm pleased with you, Mr Holywell. Here's a token of my appreciation." He coolly handed over a bulging package containing £20,000. He had never been so relieved to part with money. "I have another job for you, which will test your organisational skills, but I'll give you a few days to enjoy your well-merited gains."

Aitken had been pleased with how smoothly his plan had gone, and as he sat in his chambers, sipping on a cognac, he couldn't help but feel a sense of power and control. The death of Sir Charles Mandeville had sent shockwaves through the political world, and Aitken revelled in the chaos that it caused.

But now it was time for him to focus on his next plan.

He picked up the secure mobile phone and dialled Holywell's number. The phone rang twice before being answered with a gruff "Hello."

"It's me," Aitken said simply.

"Ah, Sir Dominic. What can I do for you?"

"I have another job for you," Aitken replied coolly. "This one will require a bit more finesse and organisation."

Holywell let out a low chuckle. "Sounds like my kind of challenge."

"I need you to find someone who will organise a gang of youths to carry out random killings on the streets of London as happened in January and February. This person will be answerable to only you, but he will have to be too scared to ever betray you, clear? The youths will be paid £200 per killing—I want this campaign to start in April. He will make them aware of CCTV surveillance and how to remain undetected. Can it be done?"

"Of course, but what will he receive?"

"£1000 a month and you, my friend, will receive twice that if everything proceeds smoothly," Aitken continued, feeling the thrill of power coursing through him.

"Hmm... that could be tricky," Holywell pondered. "But not impossible."

"I trust your judgement," Aitken replied confidently. "Take your time to gather information and plan accordingly."

"Consider it done," Holywell assured him before ending the call.

Sir Dominic meticulously replaced Holywell's phone on his tray of hidden mobiles, neatly labelled *Sandy Beach* after the large bay in Cornwall with its sandy beach, known as Holywell. He smiled smugly at his wit and the extent of general knowledge as he locked the safe. He remembered that there was also a Holywell Cave, where he had once ventured many years before. At low tide the cave could be found tucked under the southern cliffs of Kelsey Head. From the beach it appeared a mere slit, but some steps led up to several stepped pools ascending towards a hole in the cave roof. He recalled how he had had to take care on the steps, which were covered with slimy green weed, but that Holywell attraction, dangerous as it was, was nowhere near as perilous as *his* Holywell. He sniggered as he poured himself a double cognac, angrily shaking the empty bottle. He would have his personal assistant buy another from the same upmarket store. He grinned as he imagined Vance's face when the killings resumed.

CHAPTER 12
TITE STREET, CHELSEA AND SAVILE ROW W1, 31 MARCH 2025

The manner of Sir Charles Mandeville's death concerned the press rather more than discovering who might have committed the crime. This was a relief for Vance, who in this way came under less external pressure. While the popular newspapers wallowed in the scandalous aspect of the case, only one serious journalist, whose circulation was limited, posed the crucial question: who benefitted most from the death of Sir Charles?

Motive occupied Vance, who knew from his officers that Sir Dominic had returned to St Aidan's to retrieve the discarded robe. He understood that a Brotherhood ceremonial robe could not be allowed to remain on the church floor. But why had the barrister refused to halt for his men? Did he have more than an innocent reason for recovering the garment, and had there been something in the inside pocket that had indicated the robe belonged to Sir Charles? Or again, wondered Vance, were the embroidered symbols individual to each robe or all the same?

Vance decided it was time to pay a visit to Sir Dominic and confront him about the peculiar circumstances surrounding Sir Charles's death. He made his way to the barrister's elegant townhouse, situated in the heart of Chelsea. As he walked through the entrance, the air was heavy with the scent of freshly-cut roses, and Vance couldn't shake off the feeling that something ominous lingered beneath the surface of this affluent façade.

Sir Dominic received him in his study, a room adorned with shelves of leather-bound books and intricate tapestries hanging from the walls. Vance noticed a faint smell of incense in the air, adding an otherworldly quality to the already tense atmosphere. The barrister gave a polite nod as Vance took a seat opposite him, his piercing gaze fixed on the officer with an intensity that bordered on hostility.

"I must ask you, Sir Dominic," Vance began, his voice steady despite the rising tension in the room, "about your recent visit to St Aidan's and your failure to stop when ordered to do so by my officers."

Sir Dominic's steely gaze bore into Vance, his lips twisting into a thin smile that did not reach his eyes. "Ah, Chief Inspector Vance," he murmured, his voice smooth as silk yet laced with a hint of mockery. "I had merely gone to retrieve a misplaced item of clothing. Surely you do not suspect me of any wrongdoing in the tragic demise of Sir Charles Mandeville?"

Vance met his gaze unwaveringly, a flicker of doubt crossing his mind at Sir Dominic's calm demeanour. "It is not my place to jump to conclusions, Sir Dominic. However, I cannot ignore the curious circumstances surrounding Sir Charles's death and your unexplained haste in retrieving the robe."

Sir Dominic leaned back in his chair, steepling his fingers thoughtfully. "I assure you, Inspector, my actions were purely out of respect for the Brotherhood's traditions. The robe in question held sentimental value to Sir Charles, and it was only fitting that it be returned to its rightful owner. Perhaps you could explain to me the circumstances surrounding how *you* came to be wearing that robe?"

"First, you had better tell me how you knew it was Sir Charles's robe."

Sir Dominic's façade of composure faltered for a fraction of a second, a flicker of surprise crossing his features before he smoothed it away with practised ease. "Ah, Inspector Vance, always so perceptive," he replied, his voice a velvet whisper that seemed to fill the room. "I must confess, I had my suspicions when I saw the intricate embroidery on the hem of the robe. Sir Charles was known for his particular tastes, after all."

Vance studied Sir Dominic closely, noting the slight tremor in his hands that belied his calm demeanour. "So, you are saying that you recognised the robe by its unique embellishments," Vance said, more as a statement than a question.

Sir Dominic inclined his head gracefully. "Indeed, Inspector. The Brotherhood takes great pride in the craftsmanship and individuality of each ceremonial garment. It is not difficult to discern one from another for those familiar with our traditions."

A gnawing feeling of doubt tugged at Vance's mind as he digested this information, but as if at a flick of a switch, his mind illuminated. "Why, that can't be true, Sir Dominic; otherwise, the brothers would not go to the trouble of disguising their identity under hoods and behind false names. Don't you think your failure to stop on a police command and your obvious lies to me combine to create an impression of guilt?"

The barrister leant forward in his armchair, like a tiger about to spring, complete with snarl. "You had better be careful what you are insinuating, my good man. I have friends in high places, including your lady commissioner."

"Threatening me now, are you? You should know that my mobile is recording our conversation."

"Don't presume to instruct me in law, Chief Inspector. You know as well as I that a secretive recording has no value in a court of law."

"So, you assume that is where you'll end up… very interesting! Where were you on the afternoon of Sir Charles's death?"

"Ha! How can I answer?" The barrister's eyes flashed with a brief look of triumph. "Until you inform me of the hour of the poor chap's decease, I have no idea. At best, I can answer, *'Oh, here and there.'*"

"I'm sure I could beat you at chess, King's Counsel, but tell me, why did you seek to eliminate Sir Charles?"

The barrister's stare was one of undisguised hatred; he was not used to losing debates. "You still haven't told me how you came to be in possession of Sir Charles's gown."

"I don't need to answer your questions, Sir Dominic. I'm not the one suspected of murder."

The barrister threw back his head and guffawed. "You clown! You cannot suspect a KC of the murder of one of his parliamentary colleagues. That's enough! I'm drawing this meeting to a close and at the same time warning you amicably to back off, Detective Chief Inspector, or next time we meet, I might address you with a much lower rank."

The barrister stood up abruptly, his tall frame blocking the light from the window behind him. His eyes bored into the Chief Inspector's, filled with a mix of arrogance and disdain.

"As much as I've enjoyed this little *tête-à-tête*, I have more pressing matters to attend to than listening to your baseless accusations," Sir Dominic sneered, adjusting the cuffs of his expensive suit. "Rest assured, Chief Inspector, when all is said and done, you will find yourself on the losing end of this game you so boldly attempt to play."

With one last contemptuous glance, the barrister turned on his heel and swept out of the room, leaving the Chief Inspector seething with frustration. As the door closed behind Sir Dominic, a chilling realisation settled over the detective—this case was far from over, and he had just ruffled the surface of a web of deceit and betrayal that extended far beyond what he had ever imagined.

The Chief Inspector sat back in his chair, contemplating the barrister's words. He knew Sir Dominic was a formidable adversary, with his sharp mind and influential connections. But the

Chief Inspector was not one to back down from a challenge, especially when it involved solving a murder.

As he looked around the room, his gaze fell upon the gown draped over the back of a chair. It was a key piece of evidence, one that could potentially unlock the mystery surrounding Sir Charles's death. With a grim expression, he rose from his seat and approached the gown. Was it the barrister's or Sir Charles's? He took a quick snap of it with his smartphone and, without any intention of removing it from the premises without authorisation, inspected it closely. That was when he discovered the tailor's label, and he photographed that too. He would visit Messrs Hargreaves and Jenks, bespoke tailors of Savile Row, on his way back to New Scotland Yard. The tailors and the police headquarters were both in Westminster City. On foot, they were only a mile apart.

Vance entered the tailors' premises and gazed enviously at the suits hanging on mannequins. He wouldn't have minded a pair of elegant shoes either, but wasn't prepared to pay their prices. The local shopping centre met most of his needs, and he had never cut anything but a smart figure. The trick was to take the trouble to keep well-polished shoes.

A myopic, bespectacled assistant appeared.

"How can I be of assistance, sir?"

Vance whipped out his warrant card and said, "I'm investigating a murder, so any help you can give me will be appreciated."

The poor man paled and stuttered, "I-I have no knowledge of a murder, Chief Inspector."

"Of course not," Vance smiled to reassure him. "But your knowledge of sartorial matters may be crucial."

"Ah, in that case…" He recovered. "What would you like to know?"

"In the last few days, has anyone brought you a ceremonial robe with embroidered symbols, enquiring about who it was made for?" To be quite certain, he produced his mobile and brought up the image of the gown. He could see the light of recognition in the man's eyes behind the thick lenses of his glasses.

"Let me think. It would have been Tuesday afternoon. A very respectable gentleman brought in that very robe."

"Do you have any idea who he was?"

"Oh, yes, indeed. You see, I measured the gentleman for a suit myself. He left his calling card and, I must say, I was very impressed. It's not every day we have a KC on the premises…"

"Nor a Detective Chief Inspector, I suppose?"

"Ha-ha! Indeed not. But let me see… ah, yes, I stapled it into the order book. Here!" He spun the book on the glass-topped counter, and Vance peered at the embossed calling card: Sir Dominic Aitken KC. "Yes, Sir Dominic is as smooth as silk," he said, a play on words since in London everyone knew that a *Silk* was a barrister.

"Yes! A very fine gentleman. I was just stitching his suit. It should be ready for tomorrow afternoon at the latest."

The shop was filled with neatly displayed suits and fabrics, all organised and made to perfection. The glass-topped counter reflected the light, making it sparkle against the polished wood. The calling card in the book was embossed in gold and had a sophisticated design. The police officer's suit was impeccably tailored and matched his professional demeanour.

The tailor, Mr Hargreaves, was a wiry and cheerful man with twinkling blue eyes and a neatly trimmed moustache. His workroom was cluttered but organised, with bolts of fabric stacked on shelves and rolls of thread hanging from hooks. A clock on the wall ticked steadily as they spoke. On the counter in front of Vance lay a perfectly tailored suit in deep navy blue, ready for its owner to collect.

"You've been very helpful, Mr… er?"

"Hargreaves, great-grandson of our founder Joshua Hargreaves. My name's Jacob—"

"A fine name, Mr Hargreaves," the police officer smiled.

"Don't be alarmed, but further down the line, you may have to give evidence in court about that blessed robe. For now, not a word to Sir Dominic about my visit here today. That's very important, understood?"

"Oh, yes, Chief Inspector. Oh dear, oh dear!"

"Don't be upset. You aren't in any trouble. Let's see... maybe you could sell me a silk tie to match my suit."

The tailor's shop was filled with the scent of freshly cut cloth, leather, and the faint aroma of tobacco. It was a comforting smell, one that reminded Chief Inspector Vance of his grandfather's workroom. His grandfather had also been a tailor.

The slightly hunched figure of the small man sprang into efficient action. "You should consider one of our imported Italian ties. We are in partnership with Damiano Presta of Rome. He made ties for Signor Berlusconi, you know."

"But I'm not a millionaire," Vance protested.

"Don't worry, Chief Inspector, I'll give you a hefty discount. I'm sure a person in your position will be a walking advertisement for our company!"

He pulled a shallow drawer forward, and Vance saw a complete range of neatly rolled silk ties, each of striking, tasteful pattern. Suddenly, he was glad he had asked.

"These are all Seven Folds Ties and are made entirely by hand and sewn exclusively with Gütermann thread. Ah, here, what about this one? A discreet blue basic pattern that will blend perfectly with your grey worsted, sir. At the same time, it makes a bold and refined statement." The cheerful little fellow handed Vance the tie, and his first instinct was to look at the lining and label, where he read: *Damiano Presta, Made in Italy.*

"It's lovely, but can I afford it?"

"It should retail at £135, but I'll let you have it for £50, Chief Inspector. I've explained why."

"I'm very grateful. It's a lovely article."

"Why don't you put it on? The mirror is over there."

He posed like a proud peacock for two minutes, then willingly paid with his debit card.

He left Savile Row in high spirits and returned the short distance to New Scotland Yard. Once within that building, he handed his phone to Max Wright and asked for A4-size colour prints of the two photos he'd taken in the barrister's house. They could be useful exhibits in court and, meanwhile, would add to his growing case file.

CHAPTER 13
NEW SCOTLAND YARD, WESTMINSTER, 2ND APRIL 2025

Shepherd, who had studied the report provided by Dr Tremethyk, the Chief Medical Officer, made the short trip to Vance's office.

"Jacob, according to Francis, Mandeville's time of death was between 2 and 3 pm, which means that Aitken has a cast-iron alibi as he was in court, doing his thing at that time."

"Our suave barrister is totally incapable of cutting someone's throat, Brittany, but utterly capable of hiring a hitman to do the dirty work for him."

Vance's desk phone leapt with its strident ringtone and earned itself a savage glare from Shepherd's deep blue eyes. She put a hand on her chest to make sure her heartbeat was returning to normal.

Shepherd's eyes widened when Vance spoke into the receiver: "Yes, boss, I'll be straight up." She wondered what the Commissioner wanted of her colleague.

Vance hung up the phone and turned to Shepherd, a look of concern crossing her face. "The Commissioner wants us both up in her office," he said, gesturing for Shepherd to follow him out of the room. As they made their way to the top floor of the building, Shepherd couldn't shake off the feeling of unease settling in her stomach. The Commissioner was known for her no-nonsense demeanour and sharp intuition, and if she was calling them up personally, it could only mean trouble.

When they entered her office, Aalia Phadkar was standing by the window, staring out at the city below. She turned to face them as they approached, her expression unreadable. "Shepherd, Vance," she began, her voice grave. "We have a new development in the Mandeville case."

Shepherd's heart skipped a beat as she waited for her to continue. The Commissioner's next words would shape the course of their investigation and possibly lead them one step closer to unravelling the intricate case. She continued, "Jacob, I've received a serious complaint as to your behaviour from none other than a King's Counsel."

"Sir Dominic Aitken, ma'am. I'd stake my career that he's behind Sir Charles's murder, and I'm within a whisker of proving it."

"It's your career that's of interest to me now, Jacob, and that's why I've called you both up here. You are too valuable an asset to lose, so I'm taking you off the case and handing it to you, Brittany. Now, both of you, back off from Sir Dominic, or I'll be helpless to protect you."

"The Establishment strikes again," Vance murmured through gritted teeth, but the Commissioner had turned her back on him to stare again at the view.

Shepherd felt a wave of conflicting emotions wash over her as the implications of Phadkar's words settled in. She was being handed the reins of the high-profile Mandeville case, a responsibility she knew would come with its own set of challenges and dangers. But she also couldn't shake off the nagging feeling of unease at the sudden removal of her friend from the investigation. There was more at play here than met the eye, and Shepherd vowed to uncover the truth, not just for justice but also for her colleague.

As Vance clenched his jaw in frustration, Shepherd

exchanged a quick glance with him before turning her attention back to Commissioner Phadkar. "Understood, ma'am. I'll do everything in my power to bring justice to Sir Charles Mandeville and see this case through to the end," she said firmly.

The Commissioner nodded in approval, her expression softening slightly. "I trust your abilities, Shepherd. Keep me updated on any significant developments, and remember, I have a network of contacts that can assist you if needed. This case is delicate; try not to ruffle Aitken's feathers—tread carefully." Shepherd nodded in gratitude, feeling a glimmer of relief at the Commissioner's support.

As they left her office, Vance turned to Shepherd with a determined look in his eyes. "I may be off the case officially, but I won't stop digging for the truth. We need to stay one step ahead of Aitken if we're going to bring him down." Shepherd nodded in agreement, knowing that their partnership was far from over. Together, they would uncover the truth underlying Sir Charles Mandeville's murder and ensure that justice prevailed, no matter what obstacles stood in their way.

Their steps echoed down the hallway as they made their way back to Vance's office, the implications of the new development hanging in the air between them. Vance broke the silence first as they settled back into their seats, his voice low but determined. "We can't let this setback deter us, Brittany. The truth is still out there, waiting to be uncovered. I'll start by telling you what I've found out on Savile Row."

Shepherd tilted her head in agreement, her mind already racing with new leads and angles to explore now that she was officially leading the investigation. "We'll need to work twice as hard now that we're up against not only Aitken but also under the Commissioner's watchful eye," she said, her tone resolute.

Vance leant back in his chair, a thoughtful expression crossing his features. "I have a contact who might have some valuable information on Aitken's dealings. It's a risk reaching out to them, but it could be our best shot at getting ahead of the game."

Shepherd's eyes lit up at the possibility of a breakthrough. "Let's not waste any time, Jacob. We need all the information we can get to take down Aitken and bring justice to Mandeville." With a conspiratorial look of determination, they both knew the stakes were higher now than ever before.

Vance picked up the phone and dialled the number of his contact, a former client who had connections in the underworld. As the phone rang, Shepherd could feel the tension building in the room, each ring echoing like a countdown to a crucial moment in their investigation.

Finally, a gruff voice answered at the other end. Vance wasted no time getting to the point. "It's Vance. I need your help with something big." There was a pause, followed by a low chuckle. "I knew you'd come calling eventually, Inspector. What do you need?"

Shepherd caught her breath, leant in closer, her heart pounding with anticipation. This could be the break they had been waiting for, the piece of the puzzle that would finally lead them to the truth behind Sir Charles Mandeville's murder. As Vance began to speak in hushed tones, Shepherd felt a surge of hope. They were a team, united in their pursuit of justice, and nothing would stand in their way.

The conversation with his contact lasted longer than expected, as they exchanged cryptic information and made plans to meet in person to discuss further details. When Vance finally hung up the phone, a spark of excitement gleamed in his eyes.

"We have a meeting set up with Paddy tomorrow night at The Black Swan," he announced, referring to a notorious underground bar known for its seedy clientele and illicit dealings. "He claims to have insider information on Aitken's operations."

Shepherd agreed, her mind already racing with the possibilities that this new lead could bring. "We need to be cautious, Jacob. Aitken is a dangerous man. Is your face known at The Black Swan?"

"Believe me, I've never crossed the threshold. That's likely why Paddy Branigan chose it."

"How reliable is this Branigan?"

"I've trusted him in the past, and he's never let me down; plus, between you and me, I've been known to bend the rules a little in his favour on occasion."

"Mmm, knowing you to be a stickler, this Branigan must be very valuable to Scotland Yard. So, it looks like we have an appointment over a drink or two." She smiled, knowing Jacob's love of real ale.

The following day, hours before going to the Black Swan, Vance and Shepherd hatched a plan. Knowing that many criminals had a sixth sense regarding the presence of police officers, they decided to act a charade. Although both were deeply in love with their respective partners, they would simulate a cheating couple, which would explain their presence in an out-of-the-way pub far from indiscreet eyes. Half an hour before the appointment with Branigan, they entered the pub, Vance's arm around Brittany's waist, and she pressing close against his flank.

They quickly located the most secluded corner table, keeping their heads on a swivel as they settled in. Every pair of eyes in the bar seemed to be trained on them, suspicious and curious about the two outsiders who had just walked in.

Vance's hand sought out Shepherd's under the table, gripping it tightly as he leaned in close. He planted a chaste kiss on her cheek before rising with a confident swagger and making his way to the bar.

As they waited for their drinks, Vance and Shepherd maintained their façade of a happy couple deeply in love. They whispered and giggled like teenagers, drawing the attention of some of the other patrons, who watched with longing or disdain. It was a dangerous game they were playing, but one that might just help them blend in with the unsavoury crowd that frequented this place.

At the bar, Vance ordered a pint of craft ale for himself and a pina colada for Brittany. Another customer at the bar shot him a knowing grin and winked, as if approving of their taboo relationship. Vance returned the smile and turned to ask, "What are you having?"

"Same as you, mate," came the easy reply.

With a subtle nod of gratitude to his new ally, Vance could feel some of the tension dissipate in the busy bar. He paid for their drinks and carefully carried them back to their table, ready to continue their charade with newfound confidence.

"Cool," whispered Shepherd, moving her head so close to his that her short, dark hair brushed his forehead, "bloody clever. It makes me wonder how many other girls you've brought here."

"Oh, hundreds," he laughed, and she giggled. By now, their presence as amorous lovers was accepted, and most patrons had lost interest in them, although one or two still watched their antics.

"Liar!" she giggled again and winked at him. "You said you'd never been in here before."

"Oh, foiled again. You've caught me out! Let's sit back and enjoy our drinks before Paddy shows up."

They clinked glasses before taking sips. The craft ale was rich and flavourful, while the pina colada was sweet and refreshing. As they chatted and joked, Vance kept an eye out for Paddy Branigan's arrival.

He gulped down his pint, and she sipped delicately through a straw.

"This is good," she whispered close to his ear. "It almost makes me want to join the criminal fraternity and make this my local."

He caressed her dark faux bob and excused himself as he went to get another pint.

The man whom he had bought a pint for said, "Hey-up, mate, don't take it amiss, but your lady friend's a bit of a bobby dazzler."

"Nobody can fault my taste in women and ale," he chuckled,

thinking, *You're right, she's a bobby!* He was well aware that the clientele had hushed to gauge his response to provocation, and he had passed with flying colours, as confirmed by the chuckle from the customer at the bar.

"Not exactly the possessive, jealous type, are you, Vance?" Shepherd teased.

After about ten minutes, a burly man with a thick Irish accent approached their table. "Hello there," he said with a grin, pulling out a chair to join them. "Jacob Vance, I presume?"

Vance nodded, his face serious now as he introduced Shepherd ambiguously as his partner Brittany. Branigan raised an eyebrow but didn't comment on their relationship.

"I hear you're looking for information on Aitken," he said in a low voice once he was seated.

"That's right," Vance replied eagerly. "We believe he may have had something to do with Sir Charles Mandeville's murder."

Branigan whistled under his breath. "No flies on you, Jacob. I can't promise anything, but I might know someone who can help you."

He leaned in closer and began speaking in hushed tones, giving details about Aitken's operations and potential ties to the murder case. Vance and Shepherd listened intently, occasionally asking clarifying questions.

"Where can we find this Holywell? Is he mixed up in anything more accessible than murder?"

"He should be in here soon, so I'd better trot along so as not to be seen with you. You won't mistake him; he's a great hulking brute; in fact, his nickname, behind his back, mind, is *The Hulk*. To answer your question, he's a middleman for drug peddlers, organised by Aitken's cronies. You might approach him carefully for cocaine, but be crafty about it; he's as slippery as his other nickname, *The Viper*. Well, I'll be on my way. What's your cover here?"

"We're two cheating lovers," Shepherd whispered and blushed fiercely.

"Be seeing you again, to be sure." He rose and shook hands with each in turn. He ambled over to the bar and immediately engaged in conversation with the man who had consumed Vance's ale. As if in confirmation that they were the subject of conversation, he glanced over at them, as Vance noted out of the corner of his eye.

Vance and Shepherd exchanged a knowing glance before Vance stood up and made his way to the bar, leaving Shepherd alone at the table. She tried to act nonchalant, sipping her drink and pretending to look around the dimly lit pub.

As she scanned the room, her eyes fell upon a man who seemed out of place among the regular patrons. He was large and imposing, with a cold look in his eyes that made her hackles rise. *This must be Holywell*, she thought to herself, feeling a rush of adrenaline.

As she sat at a nearby table, the inspector watched as Vance confidently strode towards Holywell, his tall frame towering over the smaller man. She could see the quick movements of their lips as they spoke, but the words were lost in the raucous noise of the bar.

With her ears straining to pick up any discernible words, the officer heard only a jumble of voices and clinking glasses around her. The sound of laughter and boisterous conversations filled the space, drowning out any chance of understanding what was being said between Vance and Holywell. She could also hear the occasional clink of coins hitting the bar and the whirring of slot machines in the background.

After a while, she saw Vance motion towards her with his hand, and she noticed *The Hulk* slide a small card to her colleague with a sly grin.

The scent of alcohol and cologne mingled in the air, creating a heady aroma that made her slightly light-headed. She caught a whiff of greasy bar food mixed with the sweet notes of fruity cocktails. Taking a deep breath to steady herself, Shepherd got up from the table and fought off the queasiness in her stomach to stroll confidently over to where Vance and Holywell were standing. The atmosphere grew tense as she neared and stared into Holywell's eyes, trying to gauge his intentions. She could sense the danger emanating from him, but she knew they had to tread carefully if they wanted to get any valuable information out of him.

As Vance presented her as Brittany, she slipped into character effortlessly, embodying a seductive femme fatale. Holywell's sharp gaze swept up and down her body, filling Shepherd with a mixture of discomfort and intrigue.

Finally breaking the tense silence, he spoke in a deep, gravelly voice. "So tell me, what's a stunning creature like yourself doing mixed up with this rough crowd?"

Shepherd maintained her cool façade, flashing him a coy smile before responding smoothly. "Just seeking a bit of adventure, you know how it is." The words rolled off her tongue like honey, laced with just enough mystery to pique his interest even further.

Holywell chuckled darkly, his eyes gleaming with something that made Shepherd's heart race. He leaned in closer, his voice dropping to a whisper as he revealed some crucial information about Aitken's illegal activities. Shepherd listened intently, committing every detail to memory. As Holywell finished speaking, he straightened up and gave her a long, appraising look.

"You've got guts, I'll give you that," he said with a smirk. "But be careful poking around in things that don't concern you."

Shepherd held his gaze steadily, her mind racing with possibilities. Before she could respond, Vance stepped in smoothly, thanking Holywell for his time and slipping him a discreet payment for his information. "It's the end product we're interested in. I'll take your word on the quality. It'll enhance our playtime," he winked.

As Holywell pocketed the money, his eyes lingered on Shepherd for a moment longer before he turned and melted into the crowd, disappearing as quickly as he had appeared. Vance was sure he had accepted their cover as illicit lovers needing a cocaine high.

Vance and Shepherd exchanged a wordless look, both aware of the dangerous game they were playing. The information they had just obtained was crucial in unravelling the mystery surrounding Sir Charles Mandeville's murder and Aitken's involvement.

"We need to get back to headquarters and analyse everything we've learned," Vance said quietly, his expression deliberately besotted as he placed an arm around Shepherd's shoulder and steered her out into the healthier outdoor air.

CHAPTER 14
NEW SCOTLAND YARD, THURSDAY 3RD APRIL 2025

In the dark alley outside the pub, Vance and Shepherd huddled together, their breaths coming out in ragged wreaths that disappeared into the frigid night air. The heavy weight of Holywell's gaze still lingered on them, a constant reminder of the danger lurking in every shadow.

"We have to be careful," she said, her voice barely audible above the howling wind. "Holywell is not someone to be trifled with."

He nodded grimly, his mind already racing with plans and strategies to take down their formidable adversary. "I'll contact our team at headquarters immediately and set up a meeting to go over all the information we've gathered. We need to move fast before Aitken gets wind of our investigation."

Shepherd shivered, whether from the bitter cold or from the surge of adrenaline coursing through her veins, she couldn't tell. "I can't shake off this feeling that we're being watched," she murmured, scanning the deserted street with nervous eyes.

Vance's grip on her shoulder tightened as he scanned their surroundings for any sign of danger. "It's just because we've been under intense scrutiny all evening," he reassured her, though his own instincts were on high alert.

In the safety of their headquarters, they sat down at their cluttered desk, strewn with papers and empty coffee cups. They spread out the information they had gathered from Branigan and Holywell, poring over the details with furrowed brows.

"This is big, Brittany," he said, his voice low and serious. "Aitken's criminal empire seems to run deeper than we thought."

She acknowledged as much with a nod, her mind racing with the implications of what they had learned. "Bloody hypocrite, posing as a man of the law while making a fortune out of drug dealing, prostitution, and even murder. And if he's involved in Sir Charles Mandeville's killing, then this goes all the way to the top."

They worked late into the night, connecting the dots and formulating a plan to take down Aitken and his network once and for all. Vance's sharp mind paired with Shepherd's quick thinking made them a formidable team, each complementing the other's strengths.

As dawn broke outside, casting a soft golden light into the room, Vance looked up from their notes and met Brittany's gaze. They shared a silent moment of understanding, a bond forged through years of danger and detection. Despite the looming threat of Aitken and his associates, there was a glimmer of hope in their eyes, a determination to see justice served.

To shatter this moment of progress and camaraderie came the strident wail of multiple sirens from outside the building.

"What the hell!" Vance leapt to his feet and peered through the blinds in time to see four patrol vehicles speed out onto the embankment and disappear, the sound of the sirens decreasing as they moved away from his gaze.

"It must be something big," he hissed, reaching for his desk phone. "Vance, here, what's going on? A-ha, I see!" He put the receiver back in its cradle and stared grimly at his colleague. "A double stabbing in Tower Hamlets, just when we thought they'd come to an end with the death of Baz Holden."

"If Aitken is behind this, he must have a reason for wanting to bring terror to the streets of London."

"Let's assume he is; in that case, it explains the hiatus between the last unsolved knifing and these two. He'd have had to replace Holden and reorganise his killers. To what end? I reckon to persuade the right wing of his party to press for his leadership? By God! The delinquent is aiming to be the next Prime Minister! Now that Mandeville is out of the way, he should have a clear run, especially if this government falls down on law and order. Our failure to halt the knife attacks, Brit, becomes the government's failure, don't you see?"

During the course of the morning, details came in. On the pavement opposite the Lansbury Lawrence Primary School, a twenty-six-year-old man reeking of alcohol, probably vodka, had been found at 3 a.m. by a passing motorist, who had called the emergency services. Dr Tremethyk's strong Cornish accent came in over Vance's desk phone. "Looks like a cowardly attack from behind, Jacob. The victim's BAC was 0.15% at the time of the attack. He would have been physically impaired from defending himself. He'd drunk enough vodka to last me a month, me-dear! The assailant stabbed him once in the side of the neck and left a clear imprint of a size 7 trainer in the blood, but the remarkable Markham will have more on that for you. Ah, just one thing. The other fatal stabbing last night, again in Tower Hamlets, on the Marriott West India Quay, curiously was committed with a different weapon, which suggests another killer. Also, dear boy, this time the victim was a prostitute, known in the area by the name of Stella Wilkins, thirty-two years old and mother of four. She was stabbed frontally twice with a long-bladed knife, something like a cook's kitchen knife —every house has one. Hour of decease being approximately the same as our vodka drinker, which is another reason to suppose we're talking about two separate murderers. And listen, Jacob, the killer must have been inexperienced, he left the knife in the body and dashed away. You'll have to talk to

Sabrina; it appears he or she didn't wear gloves and has left fingerprints."

It turned out to be a single fingerprint found by Sabrina Markham's team, and she had followed up on it immediately. As she ended the call, Vance turned to Shepherd, her eyes narrowing in interest. "A single fingerprint on the knife handle, not a match to any known offenders or criminals in our database."

Shepherd's eyes widened with intrigue. "This could be our breakthrough. We need to analyse this print and find one of the killers who's behind the growing chaos of these murders."

Vance cursed under his breath, the weight of responsibility bearing down on him. The rising death toll and the sinister pattern emerging painted a grim picture of the city he'd sworn to protect. He turned to Shepherd, his eyes hard with determination.

"We need to stop Aitken before more innocent lives are lost," Vance declared, his jaw set in grim resolve. "We can't let him manipulate the chaos for his own gain. We have to act swiftly and decisively."

Shepherd nodded, her expression mirroring his steely determination. "We'll find the evidence we need to bring him down, no matter how deep his influence runs."

As they gathered their coats and prepared to head back out into the city gripped by fear, Vance's phone rang. He picked it up, listening intently as new information poured in. Evidently, it was important enough for the inspector to stop in his tracks, as he folded his coat over the back of his chair. He ended the call and turned to his colleague. "We're going nowhere, Brit. That was Trevor Hill. The blessed lad has persuaded the prostitute's killer to give himself up, and he'll accompany him to us."

"He's a grand lad, is Trev," Shepherd said in her best Mancunian accent. She leant forward, emanating enthusiasm from every pore. "This is what we needed, pal, a major breakthrough!"

Indeed, it was. The callow youth sitting beside Trev in the Interview Room responded to the name Daniel Reid, a third generation of Jamaican origin. He kept his head down and murmured monosyllables as Trevor did the explaining. "We're pals at school. I'd say Dan is my best friend—he's been bullied a lot by stupid racists, and we became mates when I stuck up for him once. Since then, we go out and about together at weekends, so I suppose it was natural for him to come to me now he's in trouble."

"What have you to say for yourself, Dan?" Shepherd asked gently.

"I know I've done wrong. What I did was horrible." Daniel's body trembled, and tears spilled down his cheeks, which he brushed away angrily with his sleeve. "I killed that poor woman; I admit it, and I don't care if you lock me up. It was either stab her or have my family hurt..."

"Whoa! Hang on, Daniel!" Vance interrupted. "Are you saying that someone threatened to harm your family if you didn't commit the crime?"

"Yeah! That great big bloke they call *The Hulk* told me I could have £200 if I knifed anyone to death." Vance and Shepherd exchanged glances. "It didn't matter who, just so long as nobody saw us and there were no cameras trained on the scene. Well, I didn't want to kill anyone—I'm not the sort who uses knives—but the thought of him stabbing my sisters or my mam... well, I couldn't bear it, and mam could do with the £200. She's always struggling to make ends meet since Dad had his accident on the railways."

"Would you recognise this Hulk if you saw him again?" Shepherd said urgently.

"Oh yeah, even if he was wearing a stupid hood, covering his face. Not everyone has a build like that or a voice like his."

"Good, now take us through what happened last night."

Daniel looked at Vance and answered shakily. "There were two of us from the group sent to Tower Hamlets. He said the others had to come back next week because two deaths were enough for one night."

"Back where? And did you know the other lad who went with you to Tower Hamlets?"

"Back to that spooky old church where they meet."

"St Aidan's, Teddington?"

Daniel looked surprised. "Yeah, that's it. How did you know?"

"I'm an inspector, Daniel. About the other lad?"

"I'd never seen him before. He doesn't go to our school. I'd say he was my age. He said his name was Mike… that's all really."

"This Mike, was he—ahem—black, like you?"

"No, he was a whitey. Sorry, I mean, he was white. Anyway, to answer your question, we split up in Tower Hamlets. I said I preferred to go down to the docks, and he was alright with that, but he didn't say where he was going."

"As it turns out, yours was the wiser choice because he risked being seen by motorists, whereas you were in a darkened area."

"Yeah, right." Daniel shivered and looked haunted, his eyes darting back and forth between Shepherd and Vance, as if he were trying to read their thoughts. "I wouldn't have noticed her," he blurted out, his voice trembling with fear and shame. "She called out to me and asked if I fancied a bit… or something like that."

He blushed, unable to bring himself to speak the crude words that had been uttered by the prostitute. He looked at Shepherd, as if silently asking for forgiveness. "Well, I could see she was a prossie, even if she was standing in a dark place by a wall. So, I walked over casually, telling myself… even if it's not right anyway… better her than some hard-working docker."

Daniel's words hung heavy in the air, the guilt and remorse palpable. He took a deep breath before continuing. "I had the knife behind my back and… well, you know the rest. It was over quite quickly, and I ran away. I didn't bother to pull out the knife. I just wanted to get away."

He bowed his head, unable to meet their gaze. "Afterwards, I knew I'd be caught because of fingerprints, and I couldn't go home. My mama knows at once if anything's troubling me. So, I decided to go to Trev, and he said that he knew a police officer who might help me…"

"And I will, Daniel, if it's at all possible," Vance interjected, his voice kind and reassuring. He put a comforting hand on the youth's trembling arm. "Listen, young fellow, there are plenty of mitigating circumstances. Of course, nothing can be done for Mrs Wilkins, except to see that she gets a decent funeral. But you, you protected your family, and that means a lot. You also had the guts to come here and confess. There isn't a judge in the land who wouldn't take those factors into account. Now, how are you supposed to collect your £200?"

"Next Monday evening at 8 o'clock, we're all to report at St Aidan's. That… that… *brute*… said if we weren't caught and we'd done the killing, me and Mike would be paid in front of the others. I guess that's to make them see that he's as good as his word."

At this point, Vance was on the edge of his seat and continually glancing at Shepherd, who understood only too well why he was excited. She was too. This was their chance to arrest Holywell on separate charges of drug trafficking and incitement to murder. They had enough to make him squeal.

CHAPTER 15

NEW SCOTLAND YARD, WESTMINSTER
EARLY APRIL 2025

AFTER MAKING ARRANGEMENTS WITH THE YOUNG ASSASSIN AND releasing him, Vance had barely settled behind his desk before his phone jangled Shepherd's nerves. It was the Commissioner on the line, and her tone was severe. "Jacob, I see there have been two more fatal stabbings. What's going on? I thought you had put an end to the wave of knife killings."

"We had, ma'am, but I'm afraid it's no longer my responsibility."

"What are you talking about? You're the Detective Chief Inspector responsible for serious crime in Inner London."

"Yes, ma'am, but since Sir Dominic Aitken has set up this crime ring, my hands are tied. *You* took me off the case." His tone was as accusatory as he dared make it. He didn't miss the sigh of exasperation from the other end of the line or Shepherd's sly smile from the opposite side of his desk.

"This is what we'll do," Aalia Phadkar said acidly. "You will assist Brittany Shepherd in the investigation, but on no account will you approach Sir Dominic without my permission."

"Very good, ma'am. You will be pleased to know that we have a major breakthrough on the case. When we obtain a result,

I'll inform you directly." He replaced the receiver and grinned at Shepherd. "All's well in Vance's world! Her Ladyship would've had a fit if she'd found out that I was already working with you, Shep."

"That bloody KC must have scared her witless. I'm still not sure how we can bring him down without shaking Scotland Yard to its foundations."

"It's a game of chess at the grandmaster level, Brittany. We've got the brains to beat him, especially if we work together."

She sighed and looked glum. "I just hope you're right. It's true that we have a big breakthrough, but we'll be up against the number one Silk in the land. I've been trying to follow the money trail; it's led to some slimy bank in Switzerland, where it goes dead. That's where the real power lies, Jacob. That's where Aitken's empire is hidden."

Vance's eyes gleamed. "Then that's where we strike. We dismantle his financial network, and we expose him for the criminal he truly is. Unless, of course…" He left the rest unspoken, but she knew what he was thinking.

Shepherd said in acknowledgement, "We need to gather all the evidence we have—every connection, every dirty deal. We bring it all to light and make sure Aitken has nowhere left to hide."

As they began to piece together their plan of attack, Vance couldn't shake off the feeling of unease that lingered at the back of his mind. Aitken was cunning and ruthless, and they were playing a dangerous game. But for the sake of the law and all those who had fallen victim to his schemes, they had to see this through to the end.

Vance's mobile buzzed with a text message, disrupting their conversation. He glanced at the screen, and his brow furrowed in confusion. "It's from an unknown number," he muttered, tapping on the message to reveal its contents. The words that appeared made his blood run cold.

I know what you're up to. Watch your back, Inspector Vance.

Shepherd peered over his shoulder, reading the message with a frown. "Who could have sent this? Do you think it's Aitken trying to intimidate us?"

Vance shook his head slowly, a sense of unease settling in the pit of his stomach. "No, this feels different. It's not his style—it's someone else, someone who knows about our investigation." He stood up abruptly, the chair scraping against the floor as he moved towards the window.

"What are you thinking?" Shepherd asked, concern lacing her voice.

"We need to be even more cautious than before. If there's someone else involved in this tangled skein of deceit, we can't afford to let our guard down for a moment," Vance replied, his eyes scanning the darkened street outside. "We'll have to watch each other's backs more closely than ever."

Shepherd nodded in agreement, her mind already racing with possible suspects and motives. "I'll get Max to work on the provider, and I'll check our databases to see if we can trace the origin of this message."

Vance gave her a grateful look before turning back to the window, his thoughts consumed by the unknown enemy now lurking in the shadows. As the night deepened around them, he couldn't avoid the feeling that they were about to face their most dangerous adversary yet.

Little did they know that amidst the cloak of darkness outside, hired minions stood waiting to watch their next move with cold, calculating eyes. The mysterious sender of the message grinned malevolently before leaving them with instructions for the night, while Vance and Shepherd confronted the chilling reality that they were no longer just hunting a criminal mastermind but also his closest allies.

Shepherd busied herself with tracking down the origin of the ominous message, her fingers flying across the keyboard as she attempted to uncover the identity of their unseen adversary. But try as she might, the trail seemed to lead to dead ends and false starts, leaving her frustrated and on edge.

With a sense of urgency, Vance and Shepherd knew they needed to act quickly to uncover the identity of their new adversary. As Shepherd delved into the digital realm to trace the origin of the message, Vance decided to pay a visit to an old informant who had once been a part of Aitken's inner circle.

The informant, known on the streets as *Whisper*, lived up to his name. His decrepit apartment was shrouded in darkness, with only the dim glow of a single flickering light bulb illuminating his face as he spoke in hushed tones.

"I've heard hints of a new player in town, one who moves in the shadows and strikes fear into the hearts of even the most hardened criminals," Whisper rasped, his eyes darting nervously around the room.

Vance leaned in closer, his voice barely above a whisper. "Do you know who he is? Has he been working with Aitken?"

He hesitated for a moment before agreeing and giving Vance a name.

Meanwhile, back in Scotland Yard, DS Max Wright burst into Vance's office, where Shepherd was working on her paper trail.

"Got him!" he beamed triumphantly. "That message Jacob received came from a mobile with this number—7549 433671—and the SIM card is in the name of a certain Martyn Rowell."

"Good work, Max," Shepherd beamed. "That's one of the names I came across, one of the shady characters well known in the underworld that I spoke to Vance about earlier. Check out his background, find out whatever you can, and get it to me as soon as possible."

Shortly, Vance came smiling into the room and announced, "I think I've found out who sent that message. I've had a fruitful chat with one of my contacts."

"Ah, yes?" Shepherd feigned ignorance for the moment. "Who is it, Jacob?"

"A scumbag called Marty Rowell. He's at the head of a drug empire and leads a millionaire lifestyle."

"Check your messages, Jacob, and see if the minatory one was sent by this number." She handed him Max's scribbled note with 7549 433671 underlined twice.

"It's the same number, Brittany! How on earth did you get it?"

"I didn't, Max did. It's from a Subscriber Identity Module issued to Martyn Rowell. We're onto him, pal! Max is looking into his background as we speak."

"Good work, partner! I've often wondered what SIM stood for," he said distractedly.

Soon afterwards, a knock came on the door, and Max Wright entered. "Guess what I've found out about Martyn Rowell! His father was a High Court judge before he died some years ago, and Martyn went to Eton. He was in the same year as Dominic Aitken, which might interest you. He lives in nothing less than a Dutch-style 17th-century house perched on the Berkshire Downs and famous for its association with Elizabeth of Bohemia—The Winter Queen, Charles I's sister. He doesn't have a criminal record, but he's in our archives, suspected of heading a drug trafficking ring."

"We're not going to rush into this, Brittany," Vance said slowly. "My first instinct was to pay Marty Rowell a visit at his mansion, but on second thoughts, we should put feelers out to see if we can confront him with indisputable facts. Which reminds me"—he pulled out the card that Holywell had given him—"I need to purchase some cocaine. Or rather, it might be better to send an unknown face to procure it. I'm sure this Rowell is watching my every move."

"Who do you have in mind, Jacob?" Shepherd looked uneasy.

"Not you, old pal. They know someone matching your description was with me in *The Black Swan*."

"Less of the *old* and who are you thinking of?"

"Your husband. That is, *my* Detective Sergeant Simons."

Shepherd gasped, "Russell? But it will be dangerous."

"It would be just as risky for anyone else. Who better than Russ? He can handle this, and it's his job. Call him in, *old gal*."

"Sod off, Vance!" But she grinned and obeyed.

Russell Simons entered the office, his usual calm demeanour masking the excitement he felt at being assigned a critical operation. As Vance briefed him on the mission to infiltrate Martyn Rowell's drug empire, Russell's eyes gleamed.

"You can count on me, Jacob," Russell said. "I'll make sure to gather all the evidence we need to take down Rowell and his network."

Shepherd watched her husband with a mixture of pride and worry, knowing the risks he would be facing in his role as an undercover agent. But she also had faith in his skills and experience, trusting that he would be able to handle whatever challenges came his way.

As Russell left to prepare for his assignment, Vance turned to Shepherd with a serious expression. "We need to move quickly now that we have a lead on Rowell. I'll coordinate with Russell and keep you informed of any developments. In the meantime, continue searching into any connections between Aitken and Rowell. There may be more to this tangled web of deceit than we initially thought."

Shepherd nodded, her mind already racing with possibilities and connections between the two criminal masterminds. As she searched into their backgrounds and possible alliances, she couldn't shrug off the feeling that they were on the brink of uncovering a conspiracy that ran far deeper than they had ever imagined.

Meanwhile, Russell was making his final preparations for his mission. Disguised as a low-level drug dealer, he would infiltrate Rowell's organisation and gather the evidence needed to bring him to account. With a firm resolve and a steely determination, Russell set out into the perilous world of underground crime, aware of the risks but determined to see the mission through to the end.

As hours turned into days and Russell's reports trickled in, Vance and Shepherd worked tirelessly to piece together the puzzle of Rowell's empire. Each new revelation brought them closer to unravelling the intricate web of corruption that ensnared not only Rowell and Aitken but also several high-profile figures in the city. The evidence was mounting, tying together years of illicit dealings, backdoor agreements, and nefarious schemes that reached into the highest echelons of power.

But as they dug deeper, danger lurked around every corner. Whispers of betrayal and double-crosses filled the air, and Vance knew they were fast approaching a point of no return. They had to tread carefully, for one wrong move could spell disaster for their entire operation.

Meanwhile, Russell's undercover work was proving to be more challenging than he had anticipated. The closer he got to Rowell and his inner circle, the more he realised the extent of their influence and the lengths they would go to protect their empire. He lost one of his trustees to a bullet in the nape of the neck. So, he was under no illusion that he was untouchable.

But Russell was not one to back down from a challenge. With nerves of steel and a quick wit, he navigated the treacherous waters of the criminal underworld, gathering crucial information that would soon bring Rowell and his cohorts to their knees. Each day brought new risks and close calls, but Russell remained undaunted in his pursuit of the truth.

As Shepherd and Vance pored over the evidence Russell had gathered, they began to see the full scope of Rowell's criminal empire. Money laundering, drug trafficking, political corruption – it seemed that Rowell had his hands in every illicit operation imaginable.

But there was one piece of the puzzle that continued to elude them: the connection between Rowell and Aitken. Despite their best efforts, they could not find a direct link between the two kingpins, leaving them with more questions than answers.

With time running out and the pressure mounting, Vance knew that he had to follow a parallel route, one which departed from St Aidan's Church, Teddington.

CHAPTER 16

TEDDINGTON, BOROUGH OF RICHMOND UPON THAMES, MONDAY 7TH APRIL, 2025

Vance approached his Monday morning call to the Commissioner with a mix of respect and a sense of vindication. "Ma'am, we have the breakthrough in the stabbings case that I referred to last time we spoke. If you consent, I'll take eight officers to Teddington this evening. I firmly believe that the suspect will be alone, but he is not known variously as the Hulk or the Viper for nothing." Vance explained the nature of the operation as Aalia Phadkar listened carefully.

"Be careful, Jacob, the organisation must never discover that Daniel Reid came to you and is now playing a double game."

"There's no reason they should find out, ma'am, and we'll keep it that way."

"Another thing… no firearms, Chief Inspector."

"No need—we'll take a few tasers, though, because the man really is a hulk, with an incredibly strong physique."

"Well, that indeed meets the criteria of taser use. Good luck this evening at St Aidan's Church."

Vance's jaw set with determination as he hung up the call. He gathered his team of officers, briefing them on the plan as they geared up for the operation. The sun was setting as they arrived at St Aidan's Church in Teddington, the looming shadow of the centuries-old building casting an eerie atmosphere over the scene.

As they stealthily made their way inside, Vance's instincts kicked in, sensing that danger was close. The dimly lit interior of the church echoed with their hushed footsteps, every creak of the wooden floor magnified in the tense silence, however much Vance and Shepherd sought to tiptoe in. The hushed voices of the intimidated teenage congregation rose in the chill air of the deconsecrated church.

Suddenly, a tall hooded figure emerged from the shadows, towering over them with a menacing presence. It was Holywell, known as the Hulk or the Viper in the criminal underworld. He called in a booming voice, "Come forward, Daniel Reid, the Supreme Dark Lord is pleased with you! I have a cash reward of £200 for you, for your excellent work the other night." Daniel hesitated, but then, emboldened by his secret knowledge of the police presence, stepped up to claim his blood money.

"Watch this closely, young brothers, each and every one of you can earn a reward just like Daniel and Marcus Bloor. Come forward for your £200, Marcus—you did well, too!"

Vance, moving to the front, addressed the young men, "Police! Cold-blooded killing for the risible sum of £200 can't be right, can it? The next victim could be your aunt or your sister. Stay where you are! There are officers surrounding the building!"

The Hulk's eyes gleamed with malice as he realised he had been cornered.

Without a word, Holywell lunged towards Vance with astonishing speed, his muscles rippling beneath his clothes, giant hands reaching for Vance's throat, but Shepherd was ready. The crackle of electricity filled the air as she deployed her taser, sending the man crashing to the ground. An officer leapt forward to cuff the limp arms behind his back. Vance, instead, stepped up to the altar, "Listen carefully, young fellows, this is the end of this vile organisation. We all know that the government has abandoned you to poverty, but there are honest ways of earning more than £200. The police will have zero tolerance. If any one of you is caught for a stabbing offence, believe me, I'll make it a personal crusade to see you slammed away for many years. Right now, I'm going to wipe the slate clean, you go off to wherever you want. I'm not even going to take your names or addresses. But remember this night and the choice you have now. Make it right, for yourselves and for your community."

The young men exchanged wary glances, unsure of what to make of this unexpected turn of events. As Vance addressed them with a mixture of authority and compassion, they could hear the sincerity in his voice. The allure of easy money had led them down a dark path, but now faced with a chance at redemption, some felt a flicker of hope ignite within them. The gravity of the chief inspector's words sank in as they slowly dispersed, leaving the dark church behind them. The officers secured Holywell, now defeated and subdued, his empire crumbling at his feet.

As Vance stood in the empty church, a mix of relief and weariness washed over him. The case that had resurfaced to haunt the town again was finally closed. He knew there would be more challenges ahead, but for now, the law had prevailed.

Aalia Phadkar's voice echoed in his mind, reminding him of the delicate balance between upholding justice and protecting those who needed it most. Vance looked around at his team, their faces illuminated by the fading light filtering through stained glass windows.

"We did it," Vance said quietly, pride swelling in his chest. "But our work is far from over. This man holds the key to something bigger and more sinister than this. Let's head back and extract what we need from him."

Shepherd's taser had been more effective than the Chief Inspector had hoped. Their prisoner walked like a man under the influence of drugs. "Was it set to maximum voltage, Brittany?"

"Well, I thought that with him being such a big brute…"

"That would have killed your average Johnny; never do it again!"

Shepherd looked downcast, but rebellion stirred within her breast. "Another minute and those beefy mitts would have choked you to death, Jacob," she said, using her best Mancunian accent, which she reserved for indignation, and he knew it. He simply shrugged and patted her shoulder.

Back in New Scotland Yard's Interview Room Number 1, Holywell sat chained to an anchor embedded in the floor. For the Hulk, this was an extraordinary but wise precaution.

"I need answers, Mr Holywell, and I need them fast—"

"I know you two," he glared from Vance to Shepherd. "You conned me in The Black Swan… why should I help you?"

"British law doesn't allow us to use torture to extract information, sir," Shepherd said, "but since there are no witnesses and it'll be your word against ours, I see no reason why I shouldn't use this beauty on you again!" She passed the taser in front of his face.

"You wouldn't dare, you evil bitch! That thing could give me a heart attack."

"Have you got a heart, then? In the event, we'd ascribe it to the stress of your arrest," Vance sneered. "You had no qualms scaring kids into killing innocent bystanders, so why should we have scruples about your well-being, Viper? Is it still set to maximum, Chief Inspector?" Vance asked Shepherd. "Let's see if Mr Holywell is willing to cooperate. If not, you can tickle him with 1,200 volts."

The villain paled, and sweat beaded on his brow. "It depends what you want to know."

"First, I'll begin by telling you what we *think* we know. All you have to do is be a good boy and confirm my theories. That way, you won't be betraying your overlords, will you?"

He watched closely as the Hulk weighed up his words. The criminal acknowledged the concept with a slow nod of his head.

Vance sat down directly opposite his prisoner and stared into the narrowed eyes. "First, we have evidence that you are part of a drug supply ladder, dealing in cocaine, crack, and heroin. At the top of this carefully constructed and hard-to-trace organisation is Marty Rowell, who responds to a Silk named Aitken." Holywell paled; the cops knew more than he imagined. "Can you confirm this?"

"Suppose so."

"Good. Carry on like this, and we'll spare you the sparks. Now, secondly, this so-called Brotherhood meets on a regular basis. It's devoted to satanic worship, and Sir Dominic Aitken is at its head. Isn't that right?"

"I don't know about that. Everyone wears hoods and robes. I know that our leader goes by the name of Caligula Loathely."

"Fanciful, isn't it?" Vance sneered. "It's obviously a made-up name—Loathe = hate = Aitken."

"I don't know about that, copper. I ain't as clever as you, am I?"

"When is the next meeting of the Brotherhood?"

Holywell looked at Shepherd and at the device in her hand. She obligingly tapped her forefinger against the yellow plastic stock containing the trigger.

He blurted, "Wednesday... the day after tomorrow, but you won't find them at St Aidan's... they've changed the venue."

"Where?"

"I can't tell you that. It's more than my life's worth. They'll know I'm here; they have brethren in Scotland Yard."

"We'll talk about that later. For now, where will the Wednesday meeting be held?"

Holywell remained stubbornly silent, and Vance gestured to Shepherd. "Just a little dose to loosen his tongue, partner." She placed the taser on his arm and pulled the trigger. The weapon sparked, but she pulled it away as soon as the Hulk howled. She looked anxiously at Vance.

"Next time, DCI, let it be the full dose."

"No!" pleaded the Viper. "I'll tell you! Damn you both to Hell!"

"You are much closer to damnation, Holywell. The Satanic Lord you worship will receive you with open cloven hoofs. Where's the meeting?"

"I-it'll be at St Luke's in Old Street, Shoreditch."

"There, that wasn't so hard, was it?"

"Another deconsecrated church," Shepherd mused. "Doesn't the London Symphony Orchestra rehearse there?"

"It does," Vance confirmed, "and the steeple is often illuminated with a blue light."

"Cool!"

"Listen, Holywell, where do you keep your hood and robe?"

"At home, of course, in my wardrobe."

"Address? And where's your house key? I need to borrow your robe for Wednesday."

The prisoner glared at Vance. "You won't get out of there alive."

"We'll see about that. I've done it before."

"Pah, you're a dead man walking."

"And you'll precede me to the grave if you don't shut that trap!"

"Let's hear something useful. I need a connection between Aitken and Rowell."

"C'mon, guv! How am I supposed to know that? I don't want another dose of that." His eyes swivelled to the taser. "But honest, those two are way above me. The only contact I have with Aitken comes through a private mobile with only his number. It was given to me on the understanding that it was untraceable."

"I believe you, but give me something in exchange for treating you kindly."

"I have a separate phone for Rowell, and it's used for drug dealing. You'll find the mobile in my robe pocket. The key to my flat is in my jacket pocket, here, and my address is 14 Bonhill Street on the second floor."

"Ah, Shoreditch again. Do you give me permission to enter and to borrow your robe, Mr Holywell?"

"Do I have any choice?"

"Please answer the question, sir." Vance looked meaningfully at the recorder and then at the taser.

"Well, alright. You can enter my home and borrow the robe. It'll be too big for you, though," he sneered.

Vance looked at the recorder. "I think we've got your permission on audio, Mr Holywell. Thank you for cooperating. I'll have a couple of constables escort you to your temporary lodgings."

"I'll get even with you, if it's the last thing I do."

"Tut-tut, such a lapse in style, Viper!"

Vance went to Shoreditch and collected what he needed as arranged. Afterwards, he summoned the same eight officers who had backed him up the previous evening. He explained that the operation was identical but the target different. He stressed the danger and told them to wear body armour.

The day seemed to drag; the long-awaited evening getting closer but to Vance seeming ever further away. At last, at seven o'clock, his men piled into the black people carrier and they all headed to Shoreditch. The entire steeple of St Luke's was bathed in a surreal blue light, its spire pointing spookily at the dark sky.

Vance struggled into the heavy robe, which, as Holywell had sneeringly predicted, was too big for him. He partially resolved the situation by tucking it into his belt and by hauling it around him and holding it in place. At last, satisfied, he pulled the farcical hood over his head and strode through the former graveyard, where a total of 1,053 burials were archaeologically recorded, removed, and reburied at Brookwood Cemetery, Surrey. Vance remembered he'd seen a television documentary some years before about the event, entitled *Changing Tombs*.

The emptiness of the graveyard didn't bother him, but he felt a sense of unease that there were no robed figures to be seen and that the church's stout west door was firmly shut.

Suddenly, the unmistakeable crackling of a taser and a scream attracted his attention. The sounds had come from behind a shrub near the path leading up to the west front of the place of worship. He turned back to the agitated voices to find a sergeant and a constable pinning a swearing and writhing individual to the ground. The sergeant was busy cuffing his wrists behind his back.

"Sir, we caught him lurking behind the bush, and he was levelling this at your back." The sergeant's boot touched a crossbow with a lethal bolt loaded and ready to fire. Vance looked the man, twentyish, in the eyes. "Looking to murder me, were you, sonny? On commission, at a guess, but we'll get all that out of you at the Yard. Where are all the Brotherhood?"

The young man found his tongue. "Well, you weren't to know, of course—today's meeting was cancelled. Our leader knew all about this raid."

"Did he, by God! So, it's true that we have a mole in the Yard," Vance said, rather to himself than anyone else. His words were shrugged off by all around him, except Shepherd, who, already shaken by the thwarted attempt on her old friend, now greeted the implications of his words with a grim expression.

Vance nodded at her, understanding her concern. "We'll get to the bottom of this, Sergeant. In the meantime, let's get this young man to the station and find out what he knows."

As they walked back to the car, Vance couldn't help but feel a sense of foreboding. The discovery of a mole in their ranks was a severe blow to the Yard's credibility and their ability to take down the Brotherhood. He hoped that they would be able to uncover more information from their new captive and put an end to this dangerous cult once and for all.

As they arrived at the police station, Vance gave explicit instructions to his team. "Interrogate him carefully, but gently.

We need information, not a confession that can be thrown out in court," he said, his eyes boring into each officer present.

The interrogation took most of the night, with Vance and Shepherd taking turns to observe and assist. The young man, whose name was Jack, was initially defiant and uncooperative, but as the hours passed and the gravity of the situation began to dawn on him, he gradually softened.

"What do you want from me?" he asked finally, his voice barely above a whisper. "I'm just a cog in this machine, man. I didn't know about the raid, honestly. I just followed orders, like always."

Vance leaned forward in his chair, studying Jack's face for any signs of deceit. "We all follow orders, Jack," he said softly. "But sometimes those orders lead us down a path we never intended to walk. We need your help to stop this route from ending in tragedy."

Jack's eyes flicked up to meet Vance's, and for a moment, Vance saw something there—fear and perhaps even a glimmer of hope.

"All right," Jack said, his voice barely audible. "I can help you. But you have to promise me one thing."

Vance leaned back in his chair, steepling his fingers thoughtfully. "What's that?"

"You have to protect my family. They don't know about this… I can't let them get hurt because of me."

Vance nodded solemnly. "I give you my word, Jack. Your family will be safe."

And so, with the promise of protection, Jack began to spill the secrets of the Brotherhood. He revealed their plans for future attacks, their hiding places, and even the identity of the mole—an inspector named Arthur Jervis, who had infiltrated the Yard years ago and had been pulling the strings from within ever since.

As dawn broke and Jack continued to speak, Vance and Shepherd listened intently, taking notes and piecing together the puzzle that was the Brotherhood's operation. They knew that they had a long road ahead of them, but with the information Jack provided, they were confident that they could finally take down the Brotherhood and bring an end to their reign of terror.

As the sun rose, Vance and his team left the police station, determined to carry out their duties with renewed vigour. They knew that the information from Holywell and Jack was just the beginning and that they would need to act quickly and decisively to protect London from further attacks.

The days that followed were a whirlwind of activity for Vance and his team. They worked tirelessly, following up on leads, encountering new hurdles, and making difficult decisions as they sought to dismantle the Brotherhood from within. But with each breakthrough, with each new piece of information that came to light, Vance and his team grew more determined and confident.

One afternoon, Vance received a phone call from Shepherd, who was at the scene of a raid. The mole, Arthur Jervis, had been found and arrested. Vance breathed a sigh of relief. They'd made significant progress in their mission to bring down the Brotherhood.

In the following weeks, they uncovered more secrets and arrested several key members of the Brotherhood. The raid on Holywell's residence had proven to be a turning point in their fight against the organisation. He had a list of contacts protected by an elementary code that Max Wright had broken in mere minutes. Word spread through the Yard that they had uncovered a high-ranking mole within their ranks and had managed to infiltrate the very heart of the Brotherhood's operation.

As Vance looked back on the events that unfolded that fateful evening in Shoreditch, he couldn't help but feel a sense of pride. He had faced his fears and survived what might have been a lethal attack on his person. Now it was time to give Dominic Aitken his comeuppance. His latest speech in Parliament was as if he had struck a match to Vance's incendiary fuse. It was nothing less than a blatant move to seize leadership of the Tories by hitting hard on the law-and-order ticket. It succeeded, too. After all, why would the Conservatives not elect an irreproachable silver-tongued King's Counsel as their leader going into the next election?

Vance, still stinging from the thwarted attack on his person, wasn't a type inclined to forgive and forget. He made it his mission to bring about Dominic Aitken's downfall.

CHAPTER 17
NEW SCOTLAND YARD, WESTMINSTER, EARLY APRIL 2025

VANCE HAD A TEAM OF OFFICERS PROBING INTO INSPECTOR JARVIS'S circumstances, including past cases and his bank account, and a quiet conversation with the Commissioner led to the issuing of a search warrant, with the result that Jarvis's home was investigated down to the minutest detail. The results, sadly, confirmed that an officer with eighteen years' service was guilty of gross misconduct.

A connection was found between him and known drug dealers Henry Mills and Douglas McKay. Investigators discovered that Jarvis had placed an alert in the system so that he would be notified of any investigations into them. Also, the corrupt officer would tell McKay about wiretaps used on his phone so that he could switch phones when Jarvis informed him it was tapped. Vance shuddered at the thought and swore that Jarvis would pay with dismissal from the force; however, he needed absolute certainty.

The bank account helped his case because significant and regular payments into Jarvis's current account from a bank in Chelsea came to light. Of course, Aitken lived in Chelsea, but the payments came from an account abroad, based in Luxembourg. The Luxembourg account was a stage in a chain of transfers around the globe, which began in the Cayman Islands and moved into Europe, via Switzerland and vice versa. Pinning a name on the payee was impossible owing to consolidated banking malpractices, but Vance suspected that the payments had come from Dominic Aitken. That was a bone of contention he would hang onto until he wrested information from the bankers. He gritted his teeth in frustration, for although Jarvis was a legitimate target—a corrupt officer aiding and abetting people who put the public at risk, contrary to everything that he had sworn to uphold—arresting Aitken was his real objective. The barrister-cum-politician was as slippery as a greased eel, but he would capture him if it was the last thing he did. Logically, he had to begin with Aitken's mole within the Yard.

Vance sat opposite Jarvis in Interview Room Number 2. The inspector glared at him and said, "What's this all about, Vance?"

"Arthur, I suspect you have feared for a long time that the day would come when you were charged with gross misconduct." He waited to let his words sink in, but it wasn't a long wait—almost instantly, the keen, intelligent expression opposite him was replaced by an indefinable mix of smugness and self-righteous outrage.

"Eighteen years of impeccable service and you sit there accusing me of exactly what?"

"We've checked your bank account, and believe me, you have some explaining to do. Listen, Arthur, we've spoken to Henry Mills and Douglas McKay, and they've squealed. We've searched your home and found your robes and hood, apparel of the criminal Brotherhood, and moreover, one of the brethren is prepared to testify that you have been leaking information about *my* investigation into the Brotherhood's murderous activities. Damn it, Jarvis, that's enough to convince the Commissioner to instigate misconduct proceedings with an accelerated hearing. You've betrayed everything that your uniform represents."

Vance sat back and surveyed the results of his harangue: the pallid face, tightness around the hard, narrowing eyes—yes, the moment had come. "You know how this works, Arthur. We're interested in the very top of the organisation. You will certainly be dismissed from the force, but you can avoid imprisonment and the disgrace of a public trial—the scandal in the press—by collaborating with us. I want Dominic Aitken on a silver platter, and you can serve him up to me. What do you say?"

The inspector passed a hand across his brow and hung his head, sighing twice. "DCI Vance, I need time to think this through. I'll give you my decision this afternoon."

"Very well. Constable, accompany the inspector to his cell."

Constable Robin Sutton, an upright, old-fashioned copper, expressed his resentment by hauling the inspector roughly to his feet and shoving him towards the door.

"Easy, Constable," Vance barked. "Innocent until proven guilty."

"Yes, sir."

Vance smiled as the door closed. He could sympathise with Sutton. For a moment, he had come close to smacking that smug face opposite him, but professional self-control had prevailed. In his moment of triumph, he could not shake off the feeling that something was wrong. In his place—an impossible conjecture—he would have wanted to negotiate, but Jarvis had wanted time… what for?

Vance found out at 2 pm when a grim-faced Dr Tremethyk knocked and entered his office.

"Wasson! It's a clear case of suicide, Jacob, but there's more to it than meets the eye. I'll only be able to confirm my suspicions after an autopsy, me dear. I'll do it dreckly." The Cornishman raised an eyebrow. "You don't know, boy, do you?"

"What are you talking about, Francis?"

"About an hour ago, Arthur Jarvis killed himself by beating his head against the cell wall. My theory is that an ordinary, fit individual would have made a mess of his face but wouldn't have died. Instead, Jarvis succumbed to a massive brain haemorrhage. Why? I need to analyse his blood, me-dear—a simple enough procedure—and I'm sure I'll find that he's been taking an anticoagulant medicine containing the active substance dabigatran etexilate. You don't happen to know whether he had a heart condition, I suppose? The man must have been desperate to end his life so violently; he would have known that a violent blow to the head would finish him, given his medical history."

Vance, who hadn't uttered a word since the CMO had entered his office, sat down and put his head in his hands. "There goes my key witness," he groaned.

Vance spent the next few hours in a state of deep contemplation, trying to make sense of the sudden turn of events. The death of Inspector Jarvis was not just a blow to his case against Dominic Aitken, but it also raised troubling questions about the depths of desperation a man must feel to end his own life in such a brutal manner. As he sat there, lost in thought, a knock at the door roused him from his reverie.

It was Constable Sutton, looking grave and hesitant as he entered the office. "Sir, there's something you need to see," he said, holding out a file with trembling hands.

Vance took the file and opened it slowly, his eyes scanning the contents with growing astonishment. It was a detailed report outlining the connections between Dominic Aitken and several high-profile criminal organisations operating within the city. The evidence was damning—money laundering, bribery, even links to human trafficking.

As he read through the incriminating information, Vance felt a surge of vindication and determination. This was the break he needed to bring down Dominic Aitken once and for all. The pieces were falling into place, albeit in unexpected ways.

"Where did this come from, Sutton?" Vance asked, his voice steady despite the whirlwind of emotions inside him.

Sutton cleared his throat nervously. "I... stumbled upon it in Jarvis's office while going through his old case files, sir. It was buried deep, almost like he had tried to hide it."

Vance growled, "Not much doubt that he had. Well done,

Robin!" His mind raced with possibilities: perhaps Jarvis had not destroyed this information as a possible act of redemption in the case of discovery of his misconduct. Or maybe—and this was a flight of fancy—there was another player in this dangerous game, one who wanted Aitken exposed.

"Get me a team ready, Sutton. We're going after Aitken," Vance declared, his eyes flashing.

As Sutton hurried out to assemble the necessary resources, Vance felt a mixture of anticipation and dread. Taking down a man as powerful and cunning as Dominic Aitken was no small feat, but Vance was determined to see it through. He knew that the stakes were high, and that many lives depended on bringing Aitken to justice.

With renewed purpose, Vance meticulously began to plan every detail of the operation. He wanted to ensure that they would capture Aitken without any unnecessary bloodshed or collateral damage.

As the days wore on, Vance's team worked tirelessly, following leads and gathering evidence. They traced the money trails to dead ends abroad, uncovered hidden assets, and spoke to witnesses who had been too afraid to come forward before. Shepherd was a valuable asset during this time; her keen eye for detail and unwavering application proved invaluable as they pieced together the puzzle. She was particularly interested in the money trails and took copious notes. Dominic Aitken emerged as nothing less than the mastermind behind a criminal empire that threatened the very fabric of society.

Shepherd, ever the diligent detective, was instrumental in piecing together the complex web of Aitken's criminal empire. As they followed the money trails and unravelled hidden assets, it became clear that Aitken was not a man to be underestimated. He had created a network that spanned the city and beyond, with fingers in every illicit pie imaginable.

As they delved deeper into the investigation, Vance couldn't help but feel a growing sense of unease. There was something about the way Aitken had managed to evade capture for so long that disturbed him. He was too clever, too resourceful—and too damned well-connected.

At least, Vance thought, he no longer had his mole in place to hinder their investigation.

And yet, it was the meticulous Shepherd who threw a spanner into the investigation's mechanism. She came to Vance and said, "We'll get nowhere, Jacob, until we get these secretive banks to squeak. You know as well as I that they only make their enormous profits by shielding big-time bosses from the light of day."

"Don't tell me that you're angling for a trip to the Caymans, taking in Switzerland and Luxembourg?"

"It might be the only way. However, I've found something quite intriguing. Up to now, my research has been based on the firm conviction that Sir Dominic Aitken is the man behind the money laundering, but now I've discovered that there's a fork in the money trail. After it gets to Switzerland, it's switched on to Luxembourg in the name of Anne de Breuil and then moved to the Cayman Isles in another female name: Charlotte Backson."

"What are you saying? *Cherchez la femme*?"

"How very appropriate that you should use French, Jacob."

"Why's that? The names seem somehow familiar, I must say."

"So they should. Alexandre Dumas, père, *The Three Musketeers*! Anne de Breuil was the name of Milady when Athos met her, and Charlotte Backson was the fictional name Milady's brother-in-law, Lord de Winter, attempted to bestow on her in his plan to banish her to the colonies. The colonies—ha!—how appropriate!"

"Why would Dominic Aitken assume female identities? To further muddy the clandestine waters?"

"You said it! Unless, of course…" Shepherd hesitated. "Well, it's just a theory for the moment. I'll keep it to myself until I've gone into it deeper."

Shepherd was convinced that she was looking for a woman. She couldn't imagine a man, not even one as crafty as Sir Dominic Aitken, dreaming up those aliases. Anyway, she told herself, he probably didn't suspect that anything untoward had happened to his occult funds. These reflections led her to investigate Sir Dominic's matrimony. She discovered that he had married Tiffany De Vere, third daughter of the Duke of Cumberland. She fitted her theory very nicely: an educated young woman, most likely fluent in French and conversant with French literature. Was she the beneficiary of a criminal empire?

Further research revealed to Shepherd that Tiffany had a country mansion in joint names with Sir Dominic. It was in the leafy village of Chilton Foliat, a Queen Anne-style mansion, *worth a bloody fortune*, Shepherd told herself as she eyed the Old Rectory and the expensive yellow sports car parked outside.

Shepherd arrived at the Aitken mansion shortly after lunchtime. She had been planning to come earlier, but her morning had been taken up by other pressing matters. As she approached the front door, she couldn't help but admire the beauty of the house and its perfectly manicured gardens.

When she rang the doorbell, a maid answered and escorted her to a large drawing room where Tiffany Aitken was waiting for her. The hostess was seated on a plush sofa, sipping tea from a delicate china cup. She looked every inch the elegant society lady, with her perfect makeup and expensive designer outfit.

"Chief Inspector Shepherd," Tiffany greeted, reading the warrant card with a smile that didn't quite reach her eyes. "To what do I owe this pleasure?"

"I'm afraid it's not a pleasure, Lady Aitken," Shepherd replied coolly as she took a seat opposite the woman.

Tiffany raised an eyebrow in surprise. "Oh? And what brings you here then?"

"I've been looking into your husband's financial affairs," Shepherd stated bluntly.

Tiffany's smile faltered for a moment before she quickly regained her composure. "I see. And what have you found?"

"To put it simply, Lady Aitken, I believe your husband is running a criminal empire."

Tiffany laughed lightly at this accusation. "That's absurd! My husband is a respected barrister and member of society."

"Respected by whom?" Shepherd challenged. "The same people who turn a blind eye to his illegal activities?"

"You have no proof of any illegal activities," Tiffany retorted confidently.

"That's where you're wrong," Shepherd countered as she pulled out some documents from her briefcase.

She handed them over to Tiffany, who glanced at them briefly before pushing them back towards Shepherd dismissively.

"These are nothing but baseless accusations," Tiffany stated firmly.

Shepherd leaned forward in her seat, her gaze steady on Tiffany's face. "You can't deny that the Milady money trail leads back to your account, can you? Or that the luxury cars in his possession were bought with dirty money?"

Tiffany's façade shattered, revealing a well of fear in her eyes. She struggled to regain her composure before speaking again, her voice quivering with uncertainty. "But how can you prove it? Even if your accusations are true, Chief Inspector, what evidence do you have? My husband's actions are his own, and I refuse to be implicated."

Shepherd's smile wavered for a moment before returning with a knowing gleam in her eyes. "I have my methods. And trust me, Lady Aitken, justice will be served for Sir Dominic's crimes."

Tiffany's mask slipped further as she reached for her teacup, her trembling hands betraying her façade of control. "You may think you hold all the cards now, Chief Inspector, but my husband is not one to be underestimated. He will stop at nothing to protect his reputation."

Shepherd stood up from her seat, unperturbed by Tiffany's thinly veiled warnings. "I am not afraid of your husband, Lady Aitken."

Shepherd remained unfazed by Tiffany's outburst, standing up slowly and gathering her documents. "I'll be keeping a close eye on your family, Lady Aitken. Mark my words, the truth will come to light eventually."

With a final steely look at Tiffany, Shepherd turned and left the mansion, her mind already racing with the next steps in her investigation. She had ruffled some feathers today, but she considered her visit a success.

CHAPTER 18
CHELSEA, APRIL 2025

Tiffany Aitken strode confidently into the room, her designer heels clicking against the marble floor. Long blonde hair cascaded down her back, perfectly coiffed and styled to perfection. Her expensive perfume filled the air, mingling with the scent of freshly cut flowers arranged in elegant vases around the room. She exuded sophistication and poise, a true ex-debutante, graduated from a prestigious Swiss finishing school.

Despite her aristocratic origins and demeanour, Tiffany had found an equilibrium in her marriage to Dominic. It suited her to be known as Lady Aitken, and she had grown accustomed to their lavish lifestyle funded by her husband's successful political career. While she sometimes missed the passionate days of their youth, she couldn't begrudge Dominic for dedicating himself to his work – after all, it provided her with a regular flow of cash into her bank account. Also, unknown to him, recently she had pried into his safe and concocted a method of siphoning off much of his profit. Since most of it was ill-gotten, she had no scruples.

Though affection may have been lacking in her marriage, Tiffany still made time for her 23-year-old daughter Eleanor—now a successful fashion designer and model. They took luxurious trips together, enjoying summers in the Caribbean and winters skiing in Italian alpine resorts. Money was no object to Tiffany, who had recently treated herself to a yellow Lotus Emeya sports car worth £150,000.

But behind Tiffany's stunning appearance and seemingly carefree lifestyle lay a cool and calculating mind. She knew how to keep her husband's ego sufficiently massaged – especially now that he was party leader and poised to become the next Prime Minister of the United Kingdom. She didn't mind accompanying him to events and public appearances as his faithful wife; it was all part of their carefully crafted image as a power couple. And though she may have seemed like a bimbo on the surface, there was much more going on beneath the glamorous exterior than most people realised.

Tiffany's poised façade slipped away as she entered the room where Dominic was pacing back and forth, a dark cloud of frustration hanging over him. His usually impeccably tailored suit looked rumpled, his tie askew, a clear indication of the turmoil brewing within him.

"What's wrong, darling?" Tiffany asked, her tone soft and soothing, a stark contrast to the tension in the room.

Dominic stopped in his tracks, his eyes flashing with a mix of anger and desperation. "It's falling apart, Tiffany. DCI Vance is closing in on me, and I don't know how much longer I can keep up this charade."

Tiffany's expression hardened as she assessed her husband. She had always known that Dominic operated on the edge of legality, but she had never imagined it would come to this. The implications of his empire crumbling around them were too dire to ignore.

"We need to do something," she stated firmly, self-interest to the fore, though hidden, her mind already racing with possibilities. "You can't let Vance demolish everything you've built. You need to strike first, before he gets the chance to bring you down." Hers was a secret smile because Dominic had no idea of her resourcefulness. Indeed, he would be shocked when he found out—but she hoped he never would.

Dominic looked at his wife with a mix of admiration and apprehension. Tiffany had always been the ruthless one, the one who could make the tough decisions without hesitation. He knew that when she was backed into a corner, she could be more dangerous than any opponent.

"What do you suggest?" Dominic asked, his voice betraying his uncertainty.

"We really must go on the attack, my love—it's the best form of defence."

"Vance's team thwarted my assassination attempt. Now he's bound to be redoubling his efforts against me, and I've lost my informant inside New Scotland Yard: the idiot *played the Roman fool*, in the words of the immortal bard."

"Suicide? Good heavens! Buy yourself another corrupt cop, Dom. You've got the money to do that. You have to keep a step ahead of men like Vance. Anyway, an attempt on his life was not a good idea. One has to be far more subtle. Engage some sleuths to pry into his private life and set about discrediting him. A DCI must have skeletons in his cupboard—it's just a case of finding them."

Aitken held the deepest respect for his wife's intellect, and her advice had never failed him, so he engaged two private investigators, knowing them from his work, who were the best in the business. It didn't take them long to discover Vance's purchases of cocaine and, more intriguingly, as far as Aitken was concerned, his liaison with a Chinese escort named Mei Ling. Vance would not want to compromise his marriage, which was known to be rock solid, so it would be a magnificent lever—a sword of Damocles hanging over Vance's unprotected head.

After due consideration, Aitken decided not to go straight to Commissioner Phadkar; no, if he were to extract maximum advantage from his armoury, he needed a private interview with

Vance in his office. Thus, he set up a meeting with the surprised detective chief inspector.

Aitken swaggered into Vance's office without knocking on the door and sat down without being invited.

"What is it, Sir Dominic, come to confess your crimes?"

"Hardly that, old chap. It's the other way around. I've come to see if we can reach an agreement about *your* peccadillos."

"Have you taken leave of your senses?"

"Do you think a renowned KC would barge in here with wild accusations? Tut-tut, old boy, you should know me better than that. To be honest, your misdemeanours are of little account in the wider scale of things, but I'm not so sure your superiors or your pretty wife, the esteemed psychologist, will see it that way."

The barrister's smug, confident expression began to irk the inspector. "You are bluffing and desperately trying to wriggle out of the enormity of your crimes by a seedy attempt at blackmail. But to coerce me, you'll need something other than vague illations, Sir Dominic."

"Ho-ho! You once flattered me for my intelligence. What has become of that respect? I have proof that you have purchased cocaine twice. Nasty little vice, Chief! No doubt you sniffed it with your beautiful lady friend Mei Ling. Oh yes, I know all about her! In fact, the little songbird is ready to chirp outside of her gilded cage if necessary."

Vance looked aghast. He could easily explain away the purchase of cocaine as part of a covert operation—he could rely on Shepherd to provide him with an alibi, but she knew nothing of Mei Ling and, no doubt, Aitken had the escort at his command.

The wealthy barrister had caught Vance in a compromising situation, purchasing cocaine from a known dealer in a seedy pub. Vance had been trying to gather evidence to bring down Aitken, who was rumoured to be involved in illegal activities.

As Vance sat across from the smug Aitken in his opulent

office, he tried to maintain his composure. He had to think fast and come up with a way to turn this situation to his advantage.

"I see we've touched a raw nerve, Inspector," Aitken said, a cruel smile playing at his lips.

Vance took a deep breath, trying to calm the rising panic in his chest. He couldn't let Aitken win this round.

"So, what is it you want?" he asked, trying to keep his voice steady.

"What I *don't* want is to go to your commissioner or to ruin your marriage," Aitken replied, his tone dripping with false concern. "On the other hand, I *do* want you to back off investigating me."

Vance's mind raced as he considered his options. He couldn't afford to have Aitken meddling in his investigation, but he also couldn't risk losing his job or his marriage. He had to find a way to appease the man sitting across from him.

"I would also be obliged if you would regularly keep me updated about your colleagues' investigations into my private affairs," Aitken continued, his eyes glittering with malice.

Vance puffed out his cheeks, weighing his options. He knew he was being backed into a corner, but he also knew that he couldn't let Aitken get away with his crimes. He had to play along for now, biding his time until he could find a way to bring Aitken down for good.

"Fine," Vance said.

"My pleasure," Aitken said and disappeared through the door.

Vance clenched his teeth and swore under his breath—a string of obscenities that shocked even himself. There was no way that he would let the corrupt barrister get away with this. He began to think frantically and realised that there were two distinct paths to follow: one was to clear his name to make himself blackmail-proof; the other was to find clear and damning evidence against the barrister. If he could do that, the former problem would simply evaporate in the enormity of Aitken's misdemeanours.

Vance sat back in his chair and sipped a whisky to soothe his jangling nerves. His mind worked overtime with the problem of where to start. Then, it came to him quite clearly. The first thing to do was to be ready for the Wednesday meeting of the Brotherhood, and that meant going to 14 Bonhill Street to get Holywell's ceremonial robe.

Vance had recorded permission to enter the second-floor flat, and he had the owner's key, so didn't need to break in to enter. What he didn't have was authorisation to search the whole flat, but since nobody would ever know, he ferreted through the place, at last finding a drawer full of carefully rolled, clean socks. One of them proved to be heavy and contained a small silver folding telephone, exactly the same as the one the barrister had given to him. Vance flicked it open and in contacts found just the one number—the same as the one in his—the hotline to Aitken. Vance smiled grimly; he slipped the phone into his pocket, since he would scrutinise it carefully back in his office. The important thing now was to leave the socks as precisely arranged as previously. Next, he took the ceremonial robe from the wardrobe, and as he stuffed the separate hood into the voluminous pocket, his fingers touched cold metal. Ah, here was the mobile Holywell had mentioned, used for contacting Rowell. Another in the series of single-contact phones. He would examine that, too, back at the Yard. He carried the robe over his arm, exited the building, carefully scanning his surroundings to ensure that nobody was observing him. Quickly, he bundled the robe into his car and drove back to New Scotland Yard.

At his desk, the phone hidden in the sock revealed a series of cryptic messages, which Holywell hadn't cancelled. The first said: contact made with CM—interest established; the second—appointment with CM made for Wednesday at 2pm; the third, with the date and time of Mandeville's death, was just the one chilling word—*Done*. This was what Vance needed, at last, damning proof that Aitken was the instigator in the Mandeville killing. He now needed to extract a confession from Holywell. To this purpose, he called Shepherd, but she was not in her office. A constable told him that she had driven out to a village in the Berkshire countryside, but did not know why.

Vance needed her present, not only for her interrogation skills but also for her integrity as a witness. He would have to delay his encounter with Holywell. Sore at the blackmail that Aitken had used against him, Vance decided to pay Mei Ling a visit. The receptionist in the escort agency was as polite and obliging as ever. Vance was soon sitting alone with the delicate Chinese woman and peering into her alluring eyes.

"Tell me, Mei Ling, what has Sir Dominic Aitken offered you to testify against me?"

The porcelain doll of a woman gasped and looked frightened. "How did you know?" she whimpered.

"Listen, young lady, I'm a police officer, and it's easy for a man in my position to have you expelled from the UK. Co-operate with me, or you will be on the next plane to Shanghai—clear?"

She nodded and tears brimmed in her eyes. "Everybody's threatening me. I haven't done anything wrong."

"Perjury in court is a serious charge, Mei Ling. If you lie on behalf of Sir Dominic Aitken, it could finish badly for you. Now, what has he offered you?"

"Ten thousand pounds or—or... a slit throat!" She broke down and sobbed.

Vance weighed up the situation. "I'm in no position to give you £10,000, Mei Ling, but I can guarantee you around-the-clock protection until Aitken is safely in prison. Afterwards, remember DS Xiong Chao? Well, I can get you a job like hers, working for the police with the Chinese community. In the long run, it would guarantee your permanence in the UK and be worth much more than the sum he's offered. What do you say?"

The beautiful oval face lit up and she said, "Do you mean that?"

"Of course, and all you will have to do when the time comes is to testify in court that we two have never had sex together. It's the truth, so you won't be indicted for perjury."

"Don't you find me attractive, Chief Inspector?"

"Good Lord, yes! But my dear girl, I'm happily married to a good woman."

"And you are a good man." She sniffed and offered him a weak smile. Heaven knew, he wanted to enfold her in his arms and comfort her, but good sense prevailed.

"Come with me, Mei Ling. You're leaving this place once and for all. I'll inform them at reception, and I'll arrange for you to have some basic training in Scotland Yard. I'll pair you up with Sergeant Xiong, so that you begin with a friend."

Vance escorted the petite woman to his car and drove back to the Yard. He chatted idly with her on the way and suddenly felt buoyant, at last feeling ahead of his criminal adversary.

CHAPTER 19
ST LUKE'S CHURCH, ISLINGTON, AND NEW SCOTLAND YARD, APRIL 23RD, 2025

THE ILLUMINATED OBELISK SPIRE OF ST LUKE'S POINTED INTO THE sky like a finger rebuking the Deanery of Chelsea: how dare you deconsecrate such a beautiful place of worship? Vance stared up with difficulty through the eye slits in his hood at the graceful spire designed by Nicholas Hawksmoor and drew strength from the architect's achievement. He, too, made up part of the fabric of London society and would do his best to clear it of criminality, beginning with dismantling the Brotherhood by removing the head from the loathsome beast.

The Chief Inspector felt decidedly uncomfortable in the ill-fitting, overlarge robe, but also stupid, as if engaging in a farce that he reviled. Still, duty called, so he joined the sporadic robed entrants into the church. He took up a position at the back of the congregation, which allowed him to keep everyone in sight. Some of the gowned figures showed their impatience for proceedings to begin by pulling at a sleeve to reveal a gold Rolex and clicking a tongue with a shake of a hooded head. Vance also checked the time and saw the reason for the disapprobation: it was now 20:05—five minutes later than the announced starting time. A sudden silence fell over the amassed robed figures as a tall figure approached the altar from behind.

"Brothers, it is my sorrowful duty to inform you that a campaign of groundless denigration against our hallowed body is under way. False accusations fill the air, and some of our most dignified members, sadly, are under attack by opponents of our sacred beliefs. I, Attila Hateley, recommend those of you who wield influence and power to stand firm and be proactive in neutralising the misguided attempts, led, alas, by the Metropolitan Police, to destabilise our movement by targeting renowned figures, above all, in the Conservative party and within venerable institutions like the Inns of Court. Resist, brothers, resist!"

An angry murmuring of outrage circulated within the body of the church, its famous acoustics accentuating the sound. "Your indignation is more than justified, Brethren; I have reason to believe that within the hierarchy of an institution that we have always considered a fraternal ally, that is, the Metropolitan Police at New Scotland Yard, is a cancer which, in medical terms, needs to be *excised*. I refer specifically to two Chief Inspectors, who are individually responsible for a witch-hunt against our leadership. These individuals, no doubt, encourage the debasement of our society, favouring left-wing policies, including unrestricted immigration, the suppression of harmless associations such as our own, so-called economic democracy, equal rights and similar abominations! Brothers, we must do everything in our power to thwart these misguided individuals to whom we have entrusted our security. Let us begin by purging society of those depraved elements who do not belong in *our* beloved capital. We should offer up their blood to our Eternal Master—"

Vance had heard enough. He interrupted the speech with a shrill blast of his police whistle and at the same time switched off the recorder in his pocket. Police officers burst into the church, the sound of heavy footsteps and shouting echoing throughout as they rushed in. Their voices, sharp and authoritative, raised in command, startled the hooded figures. The once hushed and peaceful atmosphere was suddenly filled with chaos and confusion as officers, their faces stern and determined, quickly scanned the room for any sign of trouble. They moved with purpose and precision, their uniforms stark against the dimly lit interior while their bodies were angled in a defensive stance as they assessed the situation and took control. They held their truncheons and tasers ready, their expressions stern and focused.

Attila Hateley's face turned beet red under his hood as he was swiftly handcuffed by a burly officer. His once-confident demeanour crumbled as he was led away from the altar, the congregation's eyes following him with a mix of shock and disbelief.

Vance stepped forward, ripping off his hood, his voice booming through the church as he addressed the remaining hooded figures. "Ladies and gentlemen, you are all under arrest for your participation in this unlawful gathering. You are suspected of being members of a criminal organisation that has been causing unrest in our city. You will be given every opportunity to state your case in the presence of a chosen lawyer. Meanwhile, be warned, any further attempts at such gatherings will be treated with the greatest severity."

The airy church filled with murmurs of disbelief and outrage. A few attempted to resist, but they were quickly subdued by the officers who marched them peremptorily to the presbytery where Vance had installed officers with a register. They checked ID and took names and addresses.

As the final stragglers were escorted out, Vance turned to his officers, his eyes cold and unyielding. "Well done, men," he said. "We have dealt a significant blow to this criminal organisation today. But our work is far from over." He knew what payback to expect for his boldness in arresting, among others, members of high society.

The police vehicles drove away, carrying the arrested individuals to the station for processing. Vance sat silently in his car, his thoughts heavy with the gravity of what had just transpired. He knew that this was only the beginning of a long and arduous battle against the Brotherhood, but he was resolute in his determination to see it through.

In the days that followed, Vance and his team painstakingly sifted through the evidence they had gathered at the presbytery. They interviewed witnesses, analysed documents, and followed leads that also took them to the darkest corners of the city. The Brotherhood had deep roots, and they were not going down without a fight.

One evening, as Vance sat alone in his office reviewing new information, a shadow fell across his desk. Startled, he looked up to see a figure standing in the doorway, obscured by the dim light.

"Who's there?" Vance demanded.

The figure stepped forward into the light, revealing a familiar face twisted with malice. It was none other than Sir Dominic Aitken, aka Atilla Hateley, the man Vance had arrested at the church.

"You may have thought you could bring me down, Vance," Aitken sneered, "yet here I am, and you have no idea what you're up against. The Brotherhood is more powerful than you can imagine, and we will stop at nothing to see you destroyed."

Vance's knuckles whitened as he rose slowly from his chair, his eyes locked on Aitken. He knew that Aitken's boast was more than just empty threats. He had seen the power and the influence the Brotherhood wielded firsthand, and he knew that the battle ahead would be a long and dangerous one.

Taking a deep breath, Vance replied in a calm yet firm voice, "You may think you have won this round, Aitken, by gaining provisional liberty, but I promise you, we have only just begun. We will not rest until the Brotherhood is brought to justice, no matter how long it takes or how dark the path may be."

Aitken merely chuckled, a chilly sound that echoed through the office. "You have courage, Vance. More than most men in your position. But it will not save you," he said before turning and disappearing into the shadowy corridor.

Vance stood in silence for a moment, his thoughts racing as he tried to process what had just happened. Over the last few days, he had fended off the irritated demands for explanations from his superiors and was under no illusions that they were ready to pounce and content powerful entities whose only objective was to see himself and Shepherd ousted from the Metropolitan Police Force. He would not buckle. He had an entire archive of evidence provided by DC Sutton, compiled by the mole, the late Inspector Jarvis, still unknown to his adversaries and also to his superiors, plus the condemnatory recording from St Luke's Church, which fortunately had crystal-clear audio. He had been constrained to release Aitken and almost all the others arrested, except one or two known criminals considered a danger to society, including Marty Rowell. Vance needed time to present a clear and orderly case, which would enable him to rearrest Sir Dominic Aitken. It was only a matter of time.

Time was something that Aitken knew he didn't have, so he frantically made several phone calls; disturbingly, he failed to contact his main man, Holywell— in the absence of his mole, he did not know that his hitman was caged in a cell—and was perplexed and angered by the non-response. Instead, he turned to another delinquent contact and made arrangements.

Unsuspecting, Vance returned home, tired after a long day in his office, writing up his case against Aitken. His salvation was his wife, Helena, who had released their agitated golden retriever into the front garden for what she mistakenly assumed was a call of nature. Not so—the dog had sensed an unwanted intruder on the property, so when her owner proceeded along the garden path, instead of rushing to greet him, as usual, in a flurry of golden fur, jumping and tail wagging, the retriever hurled herself, growling, at a delinquent just as he was about to squeeze the trigger of his gun. Her projectile weight knocked the big man off his feet. The resulting shot sent the bullet intended for the officer's unprotected back high into the wall next to the upstairs bedroom.

The dog, still growling, had an irremovable grip around the wrist of the would-be assassin when Vance arrived and thudded his fist into the man's jaw. The blow was so powerful that it knocked the fellow with the build of a grenadier guardsman senseless. Vance cuffed him and gratefully received the fussing bundle of golden fur, ruffling the dog behind her ears. "You saved my life, girl!" He freed himself from canine adoration and addressed Helena, who, distressed, had rushed outdoors. "Phone Brittany, Helena, explain, and have her send a couple of officers to slam this bastard into the nick!" He used his handkerchief to drop the pistol into an evidence bag and sat down heavily on the man's chest to immobilise him for when he recovered his senses. It was not a long wait. Some fifteen minutes later, both the police officer and his writhing prisoner heard a wailing siren, and two officers, well known to Vance, raced down the path to the magnolia shrub where the shooter had hidden. They enquired as to Vance's wellbeing and then hauled the captive, glowering, to his feet.

"Robin, see if you can get him to confess the name of the instigator. No need to be too gentle!"

"Got you, sir," DC Sutton grinned and dragged the man towards the waiting vehicle. Vance strode towards the house, searched for and found the flattened casing of the bullet, which had fallen into a flower bed near the front door. "I'll bet my last pound coin that the principal behind this attempt was bloody Dominic Aitken," he murmured. "I just hope that Sutton doesn't beat that fellow to a pulp!" he said in a louder voice as if addressing the front door as he inserted the key.

"Helena, are you alright, darling?" He found her wiping red eyes with a lace handkerchief. He drew her into his arms and kissed her fiercely. "It's over, my love. Aren't you glad you let me have my dog? Amber deserves a medal for bravery. She almost certainly saved my life this evening, didn't you, girl?" He let go of his first love and embraced his second, to be rewarded with sloppy licks that made him withdraw his face and laugh. "That scene, my darling," he told Helena, "was the last desperate throw of the dice by a cornered master criminal. I've got him, and he knows it!"

"I only hope it was the last one, Jacob. I couldn't live without you!" She beamed down at the golden retriever, which she had never wanted in the house. "You are a clever girl, Amber!" Her tone was so loving that the dog responded with a wag of her tail and sat down heavily on her foot, pressing herself against her mistress's leg, gaining an unusual fond ruffle on her head.

CHAPTER 20
DUBAI, UAE AND GEORGE TOWN, GRAND CAYMAN, MAY 1–3, 2025

Vance strode through the main entrance of New Scotland Yard with a spring in his step, whistling the melody of *The Swedish Rhapsody*—the catchy version by Mantovani and his Orchestra that he'd just heard on his car radio on the way to work.

He became even more cheerful when DC Sutton came to him and said, "We've a recorded confession from the ex-guardsman, sir."

"Not recorded under duress, I hope."

"Well," Sutton ran a finger inside his collar, "nothing he can prove, sir. Only, there was no defence lawyer present."

"Damn! The defence will be quick to spot that! Never mind, I already have enough to put our *Moriarty* away for several lifetimes!"

"Turns out you were only worth £25,000, sir," Sutton said smugly.

"The instigator was Aitken, I suppose?" Vance refused to rise to the bait.

"Yes, sir, but that's only half the story. The hitman, a bloke named Hicks, was also hired to kill DCI Shepherd."

"Blast his eyes! I'd better bring him down before he can organise another attempt."

Before he could do so, he needed to secure Shepherd's safety, but he didn't know where she was. The DCI had dashed off to Heathrow Airport in hot pursuit of Tiffany Aitken, but instead of discovering her name associated with a flight, she found, through careful questioning, that a private jet in Tiffany's name had departed for Dubai. Shepherd immediately called Interpol there, but found them strangely uncooperative, unwilling to arrest the lady concerned. Shepherd speculated that the Interpol chiefs had come under severe external pressure, which was true, as vested interests came into play. Tiffany Aitken, she later learnt, had deposited huge sums in a UAE bank under the name of Gauthier Enterprises Inc.—the name of a Cayman Islands frontman company. Shepherd gritted her teeth and refused to give in. She would follow the money trail and bring the full force of the law to bear on the tax evader, not to mention her profits from her possible role as a drug and people trafficker. Shepherd and Vance had followed separate trails for too long, so she was amazed to learn that Tiffany's husband had issued hers and Vance's death warrants.

On hearing about Vance's narrow escape, she was inclined to agree that priority should be given to Sir Dominic Aitken's downfall.

Vance spent sleepless nights meticulously planning his next move. He delved into the darkest corners of Dominic Aitken's past, unearthing secrets that would make even the most seasoned politician tremble. With each piece of damning information he uncovered, Vance's resolve grew stronger. He knew he had the power to bring down the man who had dared to challenge him.

As the days turned into weeks, Vance orchestrated a series of carefully calculated leaks to the press. Scandals that rocked the political world erupted one after another, all pointing back to

Dominic Aitken. The public's perception of the once-beloved politician began to shift, tainted by the shadow of corruption and deceit. In vain—indeed, counterproductively—were his attempts to gag the press.

Vance furthered his campaign by discreetly reaching out to key figures within the party who had grown wary of Aitken's iron grip on power. Vance knew that to succeed, he needed allies in high places. Slowly but surely, whispers of dissent began to spread throughout the ranks. But Vance was not content with mere whispers. He arranged a series of carefully calculated leaks to the press, each one designed to chip away further at Aitken's carefully constructed façade. Scandals surfaced, secrets were revealed, and doubts began to fester.

Dominic Aitken's downfall was swift and merciless. His support crumbled, his allies turned against him, and his reputation lay in ruins. And through it all, Vance watched from the sidelines with a satisfied smile, knowing that he had succeeded in delivering the comeuppance he so fiercely sought. As the days flew by, Vance watched with satisfaction as Aitken's support within the party began to crumble. Scandals that Vance had unearthed were splashed across the front pages of every newspaper, tarnishing Aitken's once-impeccable reputation beyond repair. Public opinion turned against him, and soon even his staunchest allies were distancing themselves from the disgraced politician and KC. This culminated in the Commissioner's consent to Aitken's rearrest.

Finally, the day of reckoning arrived. A high-profile inquiry was launched into Aitken's conduct, and Vance was called upon to testify against him. With unwavering resolve, Vance stood before the committee and, referring to his and Jarvis's case notes interspersed with his recordings, laid bare the extent of Aitken's abuse of power and his delinquency. Vance made it clear that Aitken—as the Devil's servant—should be held responsible for over thirty fatal stabbings in London. One popular tabloid ran the headline **THE DEVIL'S ADVOCATE**.

As the pressure mounted, Aitken grew increasingly paranoid, his once-unwavering confidence starting to crack. Vance watched with a satisfied smile as the former confidence and suavity were replaced by self-condemnatory aggression and a defensiveness that did him no favours but increased the case for the prosecution.

Permission from his superiors was no longer needed for Vance to proceed against Aitken; nonetheless, now that he was locked away, Vance still wanted to play by the book. The barrister's Chelsea mansion stood stoic and imposing, as if it were guarding the dark secrets hidden within its walls. Inspector Vance had obtained a search warrant after gathering enough evidence to link the esteemed barrister to a series of disturbing crimes. He had a hunch that the lawyer's lavish home would hold the key to unravelling this complex case.

As he stepped through the large oak doors, Vance's experienced eyes scanned the opulent foyer, noting the valuable art pieces and expensive furniture. But he was not there to admire the wealth of the suspect; he was there to find the truth.

With the search warrant in hand, he headed straight to the barrister's library. As he started searching through the shelves, he noticed a slight indentation on the panelling. With a press of his finger, it slid open, revealing a hidden door.

Without hesitation, Vance ventured into the secret passage, his heart racing with excitement and anticipation.

The walls were adorned with grotesque carvings and paintings of demonic creatures, their eyes seeming to follow Vance's every move. Strange words were written in blood—whether human or animal, Vance could not tell. In the centre of the room stood a sinister altar, draped in black cloth, covered in dried blood and surrounded by various sacrificial tools.

A musty, damp scent of old stone and decay wafted through the air, intermingled with hints of burning incense and something rotten—a thick, cloying smell that seemed to stick in the throat.

To Vance's fervid imagination, the eerie silence of the hidden chamber was broken by the soft whispers of chanting and the rustling of robes against stone walls. He lit the flickering candles, which cast shadows that seemed to dance and whisper in the darkness. At least, they freed him from bringing his torch to bear.

Vance started, for a moment fearing he was not alone, as next to the black-draped altar stood a statue of a hooded figure holding a long-bladed knife in both hands. Behind the statue, and pointing towards a white screen, stood an 8mm projector.

With trembling hands, Vance switched it on and watched in horror as an animated version of the hooded statue plunged the knife into a young, naked girl's chest. His gorge rose, and he quickly stopped the film and sealed the reel in an evidence bag. This was the definitive proof he needed to bring down the sick, perverted barrister.

But before leaving, Vance took out his smartphone and snapped several photos of the diabolical chamber, documenting the barrister's depravity for eventual use in court.

Back in Scotland Yard, he cut out one frame of the film, showing the girl's face clearly, and took it to Max Wright, ordering him to make a poster of it to release to the press. He asked him to splice the film so that it could be used again without that one clip. The press release specifically asked if anyone knew the girl, and it received a reply the next day when a Romanian immigrant worker, looking flustered, was shown into Vance's office.

"My name is Victor Serynek, Inspector. Have you found my Cristina? She disappeared on her way home from school in February 2023, and we haven't heard from her since. The police haven't contacted us since her disappearance. She was only fifteen then."

"I'm sorry, Mr Serynek, I have terrible news for you. I now know that your girl was murdered. We believe she was drugged and would not have suffered, but she was killed in a diabolical sacrificial rite. I know who the killer was, and he will be duly punished for his horrific deeds." Vance looked at the anguished face and, at that moment, wished that he was a thousand miles away, doing a different job.

"Who is the maniac, Inspector?"

"I'm sorry, sir. At present, I am not allowed to say, but very soon the news will be in all the media. Trust me, justice will be done. We have him! Here, have a glass of whisky. You look as if you could do with a drop. I'm deeply sorry, believe me." He handed a generous measure of his precious single malt to the rough-skinned hand of the labourer, who knocked it back like water and managed a weak, grateful smile. Vance watched him leave with the fire of fury in his belly. He would only be satisfied when Aitken was locked away forever. His smarminess would go down a treat with the old lags in prison, he smiled cynically. If Aitken's features were left unscarred, he would be deeply disappointed—not that he condoned violence in His Majesty's Prisons.

Several days later, a public inquiry led to a legal procedure whereby Aitken was charged with murder and with instigation to multiple murders as the principal charges in a list as long as Vance's forearm. The trial of the century was scheduled for June 2025, to be celebrated in what the press gleefully called The Old Bailey—more properly the Central Criminal Court.

Shepherd was, however, unhappy. She was convinced that the mastermind behind Aitken wasn't him, as she put it in broad Mancunian, *"It's the bloody wife. Butter wouldn't melt in her mouth, and I mean to prove it."*

Her investigation was triggered by a friendly and apologetic call from the UAE branch of Interpol. The seconded British Chief Inspector, highly embarrassed, revealed that they had come under pressure *"from the highest authorities"* not to arrest Lady Aitken. He could verify that she had visited the ENBD—the Emirates National Bank of Dubai, who were prepared to reveal only that the lady in question had deposited a significant sum with them. "Significant enough to put pressure on Interpol via a couple of phone calls," the Chief Inspector speculated. "The bank manager would only tell me that subsequently the money was transferred to a Cayman Island company, but he would not give me the name, I'm afraid."

"Thanks for your help, Chief Inspector McDonald. I'll take it from there," Shepherd said with a determined edge to her voice.

Her first task was to visit Vauxhall and her contact in MI5. She had no trouble under the circumstances in having him obtain a passport in the name of Lady Tiffany Aitken, but naturally, with Brittany's photograph sealed in it. She collected it three days later and promised to use it with great discretion.

Shepherd wasted no time in probing into the financial records of Lady Aitken, determined to uncover the elusive connection that would tie her to the string of murders orchestrated by her husband. With a steely resolve, Shepherd flew to Dubai, her mind racing with possibilities and her heart heavy with the weight of justice that needed to be served. She used her own passport on this occasion.

As she arrived at the ENBD, Shepherd presented herself as a financial consultant seeking information about offshore investments. The bank manager, a middle-aged man with a wary expression, led her to a private room where they could speak discreetly.

"I'm looking into a particular account holder," Shepherd began, her eyes fixed on the manager's face for any flicker of recognition. "A woman who recently made a significant deposit with your bank."

The manager hesitated for a moment before nodding reluctantly. "I cannot disclose personal information without proper authorization," he said cautiously.

Shepherd leaned forward, her gaze unwavering. "I'm not here to play games. I'm no financial consultant, but an agent of MI6," she half-lied, "and believe me, if you don't cooperate, I wouldn't want to be in your shoes. Lives are at stake, and I need your collaboration to bring a dangerous criminal to justice. This woman is involved in a series of heinous crimes, and I believe you can help me stop her."

The manager's eyes widened in surprise, and he seemed to weigh his options for a moment before sighing deeply. "I could lose my job for this," he muttered under his breath. But then, with a resigned look, he pulled out a file from his desk drawer and slid it across to Shepherd.

"This is all the information we have on the account holder you're interested in," the manager said quietly. "But please, be discreet. I don't want any trouble."

Shepherd nodded solemnly, gratitude shining in her eyes. She quickly scanned through the documents, her heart pounding with anticipation. And there, among the financial records and transaction details, she found the crucial piece of evidence she had been searching for.

A wire transfer to a company registered in the Cayman Islands under the company name of *Gauthier Enterprises Inc*. Even if there hadn't been other confirmation in the file that she was reading about Tiffany Aitken, the name Gauthier was enough. Again, the wretched woman's fantasy had not stretched beyond Dumas, but this time, *fils*, not *père*. His protagonist in *The Lady of the Camellias* was Marguerite Gauthier.

"I'll confiscate this file," Shepherd rose, and her body language brooked no argument.

"Fine, she's paid our commissions and I doubt we'll work with her again," he said, his tone resigned and mildly resentful. Shepherd didn't care: she had another night in Dubai in her luxury hotel and then the prospect of a visit to the Cayman Islands.

She booked an Emirates flight to Toronto, where she boarded an Air Canada connection to the Cayman Islands. An in-flight magazine had provided her with the name of a luxury hotel on Grand Cayman. Normally, Shepherd would not have stayed anywhere so pretentious, but she had to keep up appearances in her role as Lady Tiffany. She presented her passport in the name of Lady Tiffany Aitken at reception. The Black Urchin Boutique Resort in George Town provided her with a suite with a sea view. The price made her head reel, but she was confident in the complete backing of the Commissioner. The luxuriousness of her suite took her breath away.

She was drying her short hair after her shower when she heard a gentle knock on the door. Checking her appearance in the mirror, she was satisfied that she could present herself to anyone. Opening the door, she found herself staring into a dark brown face with flashing white teeth. "Were you looking for me?" she asked in her best faked Oxford accent.

"Forgive me for disturbing you, my lady. The name is Ruben Bodden. We have a mutual acquaintance in Jasper Fairweather. I had instructions from him to fly to London to meet you. Imagine my surprise when I learnt that I didn't need to travel to meet you!"

"Good heavens! News travels fast on the Caymans. I've only been here a couple of hours. Why don't you come in and tell me why you want to meet me?"

The man with the long sideburns and pencil moustache looked at her with surprise. Shepherd realised that she had made her first mistake but covered it with a genial idea. "One never knows whether a room is bugged," she said casually. "Perhaps if we speak on the balcony, we can be quite sure that no indiscreet ears are listening to our conversation, Mr Bodden." She click-clacked her way, hips swaying, to the French windows and opened them to reveal a well-furnished balcony overlooking the beach. She indicated a white armchair for him to sit in.

"How about a drink? What's your poison?" she smiled sweetly.

"I'll join you in your choice, my lady."

She made a great show of ringing down to reception to order two Daiquiris, which arrived with startling rapidity. She tipped the young man generously, and he left with a broad smile.

"Cin-cin!" She opened her eyes wide and touched glasses. "So what did Jasper tell you exactly, Mr Bodden?" She lowered her voice, imagining that it would be something illegal. She wasn't expecting his reply, which shook her to the very core.

"He explained that you needed two high-ranking London police officers eliminating, milady, but with the utmost discretion."

"Did he provide you with names and where they work?"

"Oh yes, they are both detective chief inspectors at New Scotland Yard." Shepherd's left-hand knuckles whitened and her nails dug into her palm. Her drink trembled in her right hand. Bodden noticed and reassured her, "It's alright, my lady. Only Jasper and I know about this. Your precaution to speak out here was very wise. These officers are called Vance and Shepherd."

Brittany's eyes narrowed and she said coldly, "And do you think you are able to carry out this deed, Mr Bodden? You don't look like a cold-blooded killer to me."

"You are so perspicacious, madam. My job is to provide the hitmen. I have contact with two capable Russian mercenaries."

"I see. Did Fairweather mention your fee?"

The dark countenance gazed at her anxiously. "Well, no, my lady, that would have been the purpose of our meeting in London."

"It's fortunate, Ruben"—she risked using his first name—" that we should meet here. I'm too well-known in the city. I expect that these Russians are expensive?"

"I think we'll need both, with there being two targets. It'll have to be a well-planned and coordinated operation. They normally charge £10,000 per hit, but these targets are high-profile."

"Indeed, they are, so we'll double that," she said lightly, "and your fee as intermediary?"

"Well, I have to halve it with Jasper."

"Would the same sum as the shooters satisfy you, Mr Bodden?"

"£10,000?" he said incredulously.

"Each, of course."

Bodden gulped. He was expecting much less. "Yes, indeed, milady, most satisfactory"—especially since he would swindle Jasper and give him £5,000.

"Good, then that's a grand total of £60,000, which, of course, will also pay for your absolute discretion."

"I can assure you that nobody will be able to trace the killings to you, milady." He winked. "That's one of the benefits of working out of the Caymans, as you know."

"Right, I need some time to organise the cash, Ruben. Why don't you return tomorrow at 1 pm?"

They shook hands, Shepherd fuming inside but outwardly elegant and cordial.

She sat before a dressing table, applied her discreet make-up, and added a pair of gold circle earrings and a bracelet. She studied herself more than usual, wondering whether she might pass herself off as an elegant English aristocrat's daughter. Despite her Manchester working-class origins and comprehensive school education, her Durham university days and life as a high-ranking police officer had removed the rough edges, and she was blessed with a natural beauty that confounded the harsh demands of police work. She nodded at her reflected image, *Yes, I'll pass muster!*

At the reception desk, she asked for and obtained a map of Grand Cayman. Taking a comfortable beige leather armchair, she sank back and studied it carefully. Her first reaction was dismay at the number of banks in the capital, but she noticed that most of them were clustered around Elgin Avenue and there, at number 200, was the Peter A. Tompkins Building, housing the Cayman National Bank. Where else would a distant English investor place her money? Surely, not in one of the smaller banks? She stood quickly and crossed back to reception, waited until a family of four had checked in, and then asked for a taxi as soon as possible.

The cheerful driver deposited her outside an impressive white building with a pediment, clearly lettered with the words *Cayman National Bank*. She entered with the air of one who owned the place and demanded to see the manager, giving her false name and showing her passport. She was invited to wait for five minutes in a comfortable ante-chamber, where she enjoyed looking at marvellous framed photographs of stunning white sandy beaches fringed with palm trees, the sand contrasting admirably with the splendid, calm turquoise sea. *Oh, I could live here for six months a year*, she thought happily.

Soon, a tall, slim man with aquiline features, his gold-rimmed spectacles perched unobtrusively on his hooked nose, approached her and inquired, "Lady Tiffany Aitken?"

"'Tis I," Shepherd replied in playful Shakespearean vein.

"Welcome, your ladyship, please come this way." He led her into his plush office and offered her a studded green leather armchair and a refreshing drink.

"I think I'll pass on the drink, Mr Oliver; it's still early in the day, but thank you all the same."

The manager smiled his approval and immediately got down to business. "I do hope that you have found our services satisfactory, Lady Aitken?"

"Yes, indeed, but the reason for my visit is that I would like a detailed statement of my account since I opened it. I will not go into the technicalities underlying this request, sir. Suffice it to say that it has nothing to do with your services. I'm only interested in studying the sums that arrive here."

"Ah, I see! You suspect siphoning somewhere, tch-tch! Well, we can most certainly provide you with the statements you require, my lady. Please allow me to make a quick call to meet your request. I sincerely hope that you will find everything to be in order. I can assure you of absolute integrity."

"I don't doubt it at all, Mr Oliver. Indeed, I must compliment you on your wise investment of my funds. I know that I am in capable hands." She smiled prettily at the flustered bank manager, who probably had never before entertained an English aristocrat. Shepherd was grateful that she had devoured every episode of *Downton Abbey* as she was consciously imitating Lady Mary's mannerisms.

This refinement led her not to glance at the proffered printouts when they arrived, but to place them swiftly in her pochette, rise, and offer her hand, which, to her amusement, the manager carried to his lips instead of shaking it. Before leaving the building, Shepherd took possession of a chequebook issued in Tiffany Aitken's name, then she left the building having achieved her objective with the minimum of fuss. Next, she would call the number on the card her obliging taxi driver had given her, return to her hotel, and pore over Aitken's bank statements. There would be time to enjoy a seaside bar in the evening.

Shepherd had a little difficulty getting the plastic card key to click the lock to its green light, which perhaps accounted for her not hearing the footfall behind her. A velvet curtain cord looped over her head, and her assailant pulled it tight. Shepherd would be eternally grateful for her disguise as Tiffany Aitken because it meant she was wearing stiletto heels. Even as her eyes bulged and her breathing ceased, she drove a heel fiercely down onto the metatarsals of her attacker. He yelped and momentarily eased the pressure on her throat. Seizing the fleeting respite, she drove her left elbow ferociously into his solar plexus, doubling him up and making him let go of the garrotte completely. Swiftly, Brittany spun, and her unarmed combat took over. She got her man in a chokehold and, looping a leg behind him, used her weight to topple him to the floor, where she changed choke position by using her left forearm across his throat to impede his breathing. She had successfully turned the tables on her opponent.

She didn't want to kill him but was glad when he lost consciousness so that she could drag him out of the corridor, where, at any moment, a cleaner or bellboy might appear. This incident was best kept secret for her purposes. She dragged the inert figure by his ankles into her room and, panting with exertion, gratefully closed the door.

Only then did she recognise her assailant as Ruben Bodden. She made one last effort and rolled him onto his stomach so that she could cuff his wrists behind his back. She dragged him into a sitting position, still on the floor but with his back against the wall. She considered him, smiling grimly at her handiwork. Why would he want to kill her? He, who had admitted to not being a hitman, must have discovered her identity as Tiffany Aitken was fake. Of course! A call to Jasper Fairweather would have been enough to make that clear.

Bodden groaned, and his eyelids fluttered.

"If you can hear me, just nod," Shepherd said.

He made the effort to bob his head. "Good, allow me to introduce myself. I'm DCI Brittany Shepherd, Scotland Yard; the officer you were arranging to kill. I've got enough on you, Bodden, to have you locked away for years for conspiracy to murder. You rang Fairweather, didn't you?"

Again, the slow nod. "Well, you'll be pleased to know that you and I can strike a deal that will keep you safe and sound and wealthy on your island paradise, although, God knows, you don't deserve it."

His voice, when he found it, came raucous and traumatised. "Let's hear it," he growled.

"You will phone Fairweather again, tell him that you've killed Shepherd and disposed of the body. In return, I'll give you the £20,000 you would have earned from the so-called Tiffany Aitken—actually, the money will come from her account—and you will swear not to inform Fairweather that I am alive. Also, you'll give me his phone number and address in the UK. Do we have a deal?"

"You got it! Now uncuff me, please."

"Before I do, I'll make one thing clear. Break our agreement, and you won't go to prison. I'll come and kill you. I mean it. Few people know that I'm not just police; I'm also MI6, and like James Bond, I'm licensed to kill!"

"I hear you, bitch!" That was unwise because it earned him a stinging slap across the face.

"Bodden, you'd better return to being the gentleman you were when you believed me to be Tiffany Aitken, and then we'll get along fine."

"Okay, you win!" he glowered and tried unsuccessfully to stand. She stood over him and hauled him to his feet, noticing the wince of pain as he put his weight on his left foot.

"You might have broken a bone in my foot."

"And you might have strangled me to death—who's more to blame, little man?"

To her relief, the dark face broke into a wide grin. "Why don't I ring for a couple of daiquiris?"

"Because I'd prefer a single malt scotch right now, but you phone by all means, and you'll see—we'll be friends again."

"I'll phone better if you take these damned cuffs off, copper."

"Ah, right! And call me Chief Inspector until we're friends, Ruben."

They sat opposite each other at the balcony table and sipped their drinks. Finally, Bodden said, "Are you really going to give me the £20,000?"

"I need you to keep your oath, Ruben. I have to bring down a criminal empire, and your silence is paramount."

"You've got it, Chief Inspector. Apart from the money, I'm glad I didn't kill you. I quite admire your guts."

"This is what we will do. First, I'll remind you: any whisper to your delinquent friends will be you signing your death warrant. Now, I'll write you a cheque for £20,000, which you can cash at the Cayman National Bank on Elgin Avenue. Then, you come back to me and make the call to Fairweather in my presence. Any questions?"

He shook his head and hobbled to the door. "Oh, and call in at the hospital for an X-ray on that foot."

He came back hours later using a walking stick, looking mightily pleased with himself.

"It's a hairline fracture of the second metatarsal. The doctor said I don't need crutches, and it'll heal up soon if I use a stick to keep the weight off it."

"Well, bully for you! Did you get your money?"

"Yes, I did."

"Okay, now you make that call, and don't forget that you're supposed to get a hitman to kill DCI Vance. We'll talk about that afterwards."

Bodden whipped out his mobile and punched in a number.

"Hello, Jasper? It's me. Listen up, man! I've dealt with the impersonator. It turns out *she* was DCI Shepherd. I did a clean job and disposed of the body. Nobody will ever find her remains. What? Yeah, of course, I'm sure. She's under tonnes of concrete. Do I still go ahead with Ivanov to deal with Vance? Okay, leave it with me." He winked at Shepherd, who glared at him.

When he had ended the call, she said, "Good enough, Ruben. Now write down Fairweather's number and address and then get out of my sight. Make sure we don't meet again!"

He obliged, handed over a sheet of hotel notepaper, bowed, and limped to the door, where he turned, "Are you quite sure you don't want to spend the evening with me?"

She considered the handsome features for a moment and weighed up the advantages. "What time will you pick me up? You're paying, by the way!"

He grinned and said, "Eight o'clock suit you, Chief?"

"Yes, but you'll have to call me Tiffany for the rest of my stay and get used to this posh accent. You can introduce me as Lady Aitken if necessary." She smiled and watched him walk out.

One thing was certain: he had a certain rugged charm and would know the best bars and eating places on the isle. Also, keeping him onside would suit her purposes. She wouldn't forget that he had tried to kill her and, although she couldn't be sure that he hadn't phoned Fairweather or anyone else behind her back, her intuition told her that he was satisfied with their arrangement. She would extract Ivanov's details from him later. He would be arrested as soon as he set foot in the United Kingdom, probably at Heathrow Airport, and sent back to Grand Cayman on the first flight out.

CHAPTER 21

HEATHROW AIRPORT, TRAFALGAR SQUARE AND NEW SCOTLAND YARD, 3RD MAY, 2025

Shepherd went to the check-in desk early, and as soon as the ground hostess took up her position, she discreetly showed her warrant card. "When a passenger by the name of Ivanov checks in, I'd like you to signal me his presence. Maybe you can adjust your silk scarf." The arrangement concluded, Shepherd checked in for the London flight via Toronto. There was also a slight possibility that the suspect would opt for the British Airways flight, but she doubted he would want to delay departure and arrive late in the evening.

She needn't have worried because, fourth in line, was a tall blond-haired man with broad shoulders. After checking his passport, the ground hostess rearranged her neck scarf and glanced towards her. Shepherd memorised the man's appearance, which wasn't difficult because he had an imposing presence. She saw him again at the boarding gate but kept her distance and didn't stare at him.

When they touched down in Toronto, she found a quiet corner and phoned Vance in London to organise a reception committee at Heathrow for Ivanov. The long flight concluded, and the passengers made their way to passport control, where Shepherd stood immediately behind him. As a British citizen, she would not normally have joined this queue. As soon as the official at the desk received Ivanov's passport, he nodded towards two uniformed police officers standing by, one of whom had a sub-machine gun in his hand. The other officer addressed the passenger, "Mr Ivanov, come with me, sir. We have some routine questions for you."

"But I haven't done anything, officer. I'm just a tourist visiting London."

"So, you have no concerns, then. Please come this way."

Shepherd flashed her warrant card at the passport controller, who grinned, nodded, and waved her past.

The three officers and the suspect entered a small office, where Shepherd, as the senior officer, immediately took charge. She didn't waste time over formalities but went straight to the point: "Mr Ivanov, I know the purpose of your visit to London. I have enough evidence to lock you up for ten years, so I suggest you collaborate from the start. You have a contract to assassinate DCI Vance of Scotland Yard. I need to know who is going to provide you with the weapon and where you plan to meet him."

"I don't know what you're talking about, woman. I'm just a tourist."

Shepherd thrust her face into his and glared at him, sapphire blue eyes as hard as the stones of that colour. "From now on, you address me as Chief Inspector and cut out these stupid games, or you'll not see the light of day for the next ten years, understood?"

The officer with the machine gun moved ostentatiously in front of the suspect and held the weapon firmly, pointing at him.

Ivanov gulped and said, "If I give you what you want, will you let me go?"

"In that case, you'll be on the first flight back to George Town."

"OK." He slowly reached into the inside pocket of his beige corduroy jacket and withdrew a visiting card. He handed it to

Shepherd. "I have to phone this number as soon as I've cleared the airport. That's all I know."

Shepherd read the name, J. R. Fairweather, and the number and smiled.

"Good. Now listen carefully, Mr Ivanov. My officers will accompany you to the outgoing flight and make sure that you are securely on your way to Toronto. If anything happens to DCI Vance in the next month, I swear that I'll seek you out, and, believe me, you don't want that!" Her sapphire eyes blazed and peered into his. "Remember April 2023, the Mahmud Abad Olya Road? Well, you're looking at the sniper who took out Bahir Jamshid."

He gulped again. "You've made yourself quite clear, Chief Inspector," he murmured, lowering his voice, "but that doesn't mean you could take out Sergei Ivanov."

"Better not take any chances, big man. I have the means and the determination to do whatever I want." Her eyes bored into his, and he looked quickly away, making the sign of the cross, Russian Orthodox style.

"Oh, c'mon, the Good Lord has no truck with cold-blooded killers, Ivanov. Get him out of my sight! One false move—shoot him, officer!"

"Yes, ma'am."

Shepherd smiled smugly as the door closed but wasted no time in finding another armed police officer. Quickly, she explained what she needed. "Do you think you can do a light Russian accent, officer?"

"*Da, konechno*, like this, ma'am?"

"Perfect. Don't exaggerate it, though. The recipient of your call must suspect nothing. Call yourself Sergei Ivanov and fix an appointment to receive *the hardware*, clear? Tell Fairweather you're ringing from the airport and that you've just cleared passport control. These background announcements will lend authenticity."

The officer grinned and, with Shepherd standing next to him, dialled the number.

"Hello. Mr Fairweather, Sergei Ivanov speaking. I've just cleared passport control at Heathrow. Where shall we meet for you to give me the hardware? Where? Oh, yes, I understand. Trafalgar Square by one of the black lions under the column. Fine, I'll be there at eight o'clock."

As soon as he had hung up, Shepherd beamed. "He'll have heard that last call announcement for the Tenerife flight. Perfect!" She took out her mobile and phoned Jacob Vance. After a brief explanation, she said, "You'll need a tall, blond officer in plain clothes. A corduroy jacket would be good." She gave the place and time of the assignment.

Vance replied, "I'll look forward to arresting the instigator of my murder!"

"Good luck, Jacob. See you later."

As Big Ben struck eight o'clock, DC John Harrington, tall and blond, and wearing a brown corduroy jacket, walked around Nelson's Column from one black lion to another of the four, as if looking for someone. Suddenly a voice behind him said, "Sergei?"

He reacted immediately. "_Da, Mr Fairwedder?" he growled, as if having difficulty with the name.

"Here, take this phone. I'll ring you to let you know when and where you can strike. Here, quick, hide this gun in your pocket."

No sooner had he handed over the weapon than, as if from nowhere, five armed policemen surrounded them. "You are under arrest for conspiracy to murder, Jasper Fairweather," announced DS Simons, in charge of the operation. "Cuff him, Sutton, and take him to the car. Harrington, come with me. I'll take your statement at the Yard."

Soon after their arrival, Shepherd strolled into Vance's office.

"Everything alright, Jacob?"

"Welcome home, Brittany! It couldn't be better. I've left your husband questioning Fairweather, and last I heard, he's squirming and trying to pin the blame on Tiffany Aitken."

"Perfect! We'll go with that, then, and tomorrow I'll drive out and arrest her. What a hellish husband-and-wife team!"

"You can say that again! Tell me all about your time away. I'm amazed you haven't put on weight with all those five-star restaurants."

"Jacob, restaurants don't have stars; they have chefs' hats. To tell the truth, I lost my appetite after being garrotted."

"What!"

She explained her break from London in detail and accepted a scotch as a reward for saving his life.

During the next few days and throughout the preliminary hearings, despite the crushing evidence against him, Sir Dominic Aitken continued to plead not guilty. The trial was scheduled at the Old Bailey for June and given its importance, it would be conducted by the Recorder of London, who sat bewigged in majesty in his red robe trimmed with blue to distinguish his superiority over the white ermine-trimmed justices. The jury was sworn in, each juror swearing to give *a true verdict*. The prosecutor, a barrister, while giving a brief summary of the prosecution's case so the jury could put the evidence into context, continued to stare reprovingly at his former colleague, the now disgraced Sir Dominic.

He then began calling his witnesses. The first was the infamous Marty Rowell, whose damning evidence spoke of a chain of drug dealers with Aitken at the head. Under examination, he cogently explained how the system was organised by the defendant to be almost impenetrable.

The next witness, even more damning, was Holywell, who confessed to being employed by the defendant to murder Sir Charles Mandeville. He told the court the exact amount he had been paid to perform the deed and admitted that by turning his testimony over to the police, he hoped to be spared punishment for his crime. He expressed remorse and a desire to lead a worthwhile life of service to the community to expiate his sins, which included organising minions to execute Aitken's orders to bring terror to the streets of London through knife murders employing poverty-stricken juveniles.

A feeble attempt by the defence to incriminate DCI Vance on charges of obtaining cocaine and exploiting an oriental escort was dismantled in turn by DCI Shepherd, who explained the undercover operation in the disreputable Black Swan pub. She was followed by DC Mei Ling, sitting proudly in her new uniform, who told the court about her relationship with the late Sir Charles Mandeville in her previous employment and how the accused had threatened her with the same fate as the politician if she did not accept his £10,000 bribe to blacken DCI Vance's name. She considered Vance to be her saviour and underlined her commitment to her new community service.

DCI Vance was called by the prosecution to elaborate on the police procedure in detail that had led to Aitken's arrest. Vance metaphorically drove the final nail into the former barrister's coffin by explaining his infiltration of the Brotherhood and the discovery of a secret room in Aitken's mansion dedicated to the dark arts. The shocked jury was invited to visualise the movie behind locked doors, and the Recorder offered them the option, if of an impressionable and sensitive disposition, to opt out of the viewing. However, the jurors unanimously consented to watch the three-minute film. They were shown the horrendous snuff movie the defendant had in his possession, depicting the sacrifice of a naked, drugged virgin on an altar. Vance's inquiries led him to confirm that the victim was a fifteen-year-old Romanian schoolgirl who had disappeared in the winter of 2023: Cristina Serynek. One juror, a Black lady of evangelical persuasion, came out of the viewing room with tears streaming down her face and her hands wringing the cloth of her dress.

It was left to the jury to decide whether the tall hooded figure wielding the knife was Dominic Aitken or another. Vance admitted to the defence barrister that he was not sure, and only circumstantial evidence pointed to his client. However, his photographs taken in the secret chamber were damning because the room was clearly the same as seen in the movie. The jury, however, considering all the other crimes, including trafficking young women from abroad, in their two-day deliberation, declared Dominic Aitken guilty on all charges, including the murder of Cristina Serynek.

Vance, sitting next to Shepherd in court, smiled grimly as the Recorder of London condemned Aitken to consecutive life imprisonments after a long speech about abuse of position and betrayal of trust. Shepherd whispered to Vance, "This doesn't end here. The next person in the dock has to be his bloody wife!"

Shepherd drove out to the Berkshire mansion with her husband, DS Simons, as extra security, but the major-domo coolly told her that his mistress was visiting her daughter, Eleanor, who lived in a cottage in a village a short drive away. He provided the exact address.

Eleanor Aitken answered the door and, on seeing the warrant cards, reluctantly admitted the officers into her living room, where her mother was sipping tea from a Royal Albert porcelain cup. Her hand shook as she placed it in its saucer.

"Lady Tiffany Aitken, you are under arrest for instigating the murders of DCIs Vance and Shepherd. Allow me to introduce myself. I am Brittany Shepherd, and as you can see for yourself, I'm in rude health—no thanks to you. I have gathered evidence to put you away for years, just like your diabolical, murdering husband."

"You haven't a shred of proof against me, Chief Inspector. You are bluffing, and your presence here is unwelcome."

"No problem. Cuff her, Russell. As you see, our presence here is only for a limited time until we lead you away to your comfortless cell. Only cheap enamel mugs from now on for you, milady. Now, these are your rights..." Shepherd recited them with a deliberate Mancunian accent to grate on her ladyship's ears.

"Oh, Mummy, tell me it isn't true!" Eleanor wailed.

"Shut up, child! You inherit everything."

"She means your parents' ill-gotten gains. Enjoy them if you have no conscience," Shepherd said bitterly and shoved her prisoner towards the door.

The trial, in the Strand Crown Court, might have been somewhat influenced by the previous sentencing of the defendant's husband, but Shepherd's meticulous accumulation of evidence against the aristocratic lady left the defence little leeway, and Tiffany Aitken was also sentenced to life imprisonment for the attempted murder of two high-ranking police officers, whom the prosecution correctly depicted as conscientious upholders of law and order.

Shepherd's only regret was that Holywell and Fairweather had survived their misdeeds unpunished by turning evidence against their delinquent paymasters. However, she swore she would keep a very close eye on both of them.

Vance, who had not attended Lady Aitken's trial largely because it had been Shepherd's case, was nonetheless keen to hear about the outcome when his colleague sauntered into his office.

"Let's go, Jacob. We're headed to Shoreditch, and I'm footing the bill. I'll fill you in on the details there."

Brittany was reliving her brief stint as a pretentious English socialite on Grand Cayman and wanted to bask in it once again. She confidently strolled into Ma Petite Jamaica Bar with Vance, putting on her poshest Oxford accent as she ordered two daiquiris at the bar.

"At your service, milady!" the bartender grinned broadly.

The bar was decorated with vibrant Caribbean colours and patterns, from the bright red and orange walls to the hand-painted wooden signs hanging overhead. The dim lighting cast a warm glow on the patrons, who were a mix of ethnic locals and tourists. A small stage filled one corner, with a reggae band setting up for the night's entertainment.

"Damn, Brit, that's how you convinced them you were Tiffany Aitken? On a tropical island no less?" Jacob laughed incredulously.

"Just bring our drinks to that table, my man," Brittany dismissed him with a flirtatious giggle before sashaying over to their table. As she regaled Vance with tales of the court trial and her satisfaction at seeing the snobbish bitch sentenced to life imprisonment, she couldn't help but gloat about how she had outsmarted everyone involved.

They savoured their strong rum-based daiquiris, swaying along to the pulsating reggae music. Shepherd couldn't contain her excitement, standing up and dancing while the older Vance relaxed and reflected on how much safer this city was thanks to their tireless efforts.

ABOUT THE AUTHOR

Award-winning author, John Broughton, was born in Cleethorpes, Lincolnshire, UK, in 1948, just one of the post-war baby boomers. After attending grammar school and studying to the sound of Bob Dylan, he went to Nottingham University and studied Medieval and Modern History (Archaeology subsidiary). The subsidiary course led to one of his greatest academic achievements: tipping the soil content of a wheelbarrow from the summit of a spoil heap onto an old lady hobbling past the dig. Fortunately, they subsequently became firm friends.

He did many different jobs while living in Radcliffe-on-Trent, Leamington, Glossop, the Scilly Isles, Puglia, and Calabria. These included teaching English and History, managing a Day-Care Centre, being a Director of a Trade Institute, and teaching university students English. He even tried being a fisherman and a flower-picker when he was on St Agnes Island, Scilly. He has lived in Calabria since 1992, where he settled into a long-term job, for once, at the University of Calabria teaching English. No doubt, his "lovely Calabrian wife Maria" stopped him from being restless.

His two kids are grown up now, but he wrote books for them when they were little. Hamish Hamilton and then Thomas Nelson published six of these in England in the 1980s. They are now out of print. He's a granddad and, happily, the parents named his grandson Dylan, John's favourite musician. He decided to take up writing again late in his career. When one is teaching and working as a translator, one doesn't have time for writing. As soon as he stopped the translations, he resumed writing in 2014. The fruit of that decision was his first historical novel, *The Purple Thread*. The novel is set in his favourite Anglo-Saxon period. Various literary awards followed for his historical novels and can be seen on the author's website <www.saxonquill.com>.

In order to put his writing versatility to the test, he embarked on a series of detective mystery novels set in London with the Metropolitan Police, who have to deal with a criminally insane serial killer in *The Quasimodo Killings*; *The London Tram Murders*; and *The Thames Crossbow Murders*. The latter was voted among the best twenty-five independent books of 2022. *The Aspromonte Riddle* is a work dedicated to the family and region where the author lives.

To learn more about John Broughton and discover more Next Chapter authors, visit our website at www.nextchapter.pub.

Printed in Dunstable, United Kingdom